PLAIN EXPECTATIONS

K.M.Bishop

—Shellville Press—

Printed by Shellville Press in the United States of America

Cover generated by Midjourney

ISBN: 979-8-9886954-0-0

Shellville Press
a division of Shellville Design LLC
www.shellvillepress.com

10 9 8 7 6 5 4 3 2 1

*To all the sisters
(and wallflowers)
with personalities.*

1

THE YOUNG WOMAN SIGHED, A SHRILL EXHALING OF AIR, AS SHE looked out the window. "Is there not something romantic about the rain?" she asked no one in particular.

Her elder sister glanced up at her over the brim of her book. "What are you talking about, Evangelina? How is the rain romantic?" she asked skeptically in return.

The young woman turned her head to look at her sister, her light brown curls bouncing about her head and still seeming to glow despite the lack of light in the room. "Oh, Georgia, you are too *practical* to understand," she teased. "Can you not just imagine a handsome, young man galloping through the rain to save the woman he loved?"

Georgia blinked at her sister for a moment. "No," she finally replied, turning her attention back to the words on the page before her.

The young woman sighed again, this time a little exasperatedly.

Just then, the girls' mother floated into the room, a satisfied smile on her face and a letter in her hand. "You will not imagine the news I bring, girls," she told them, her excitement barely visible through her usually reserved character.

Georgia adjusted her wire rim glasses, annoyed that she was once again interrupted in her reading. "What news could that be, mamma?" she asked knowing that her mother would not tell them unless someone did.

"Mr. and Mrs. Dorset have invited their nephew down for the season. He will arrive just in time for their ball!" their mother replied as if the younger women were supposed to know the importance of what such a statement meant.

Neither of the sisters replied.

"He is a man of substantial income and is single! Completely unattached!" their mother proclaimed. "It is about time someone of means equal to our own comes into the neighborhood."

Georgia blinked at her mother, sure she must have read something quite similar to this situation in a book.

Evangelina looked at her mother indiscernibly. "What do you mean, mamma? There are plenty of deserving men in our own little Barchester."

Mrs. Hamilton arched an eyebrow. "What I mean, dear, is that he is said to have upwards of eight thousand pounds a year!"

This time, Evangelina's eyes widened. "Eight thousand a year?" she repeated. "How becoming in a bachelor."

"A handsome match for you to be sure!" their mother continued.

"I am sure it is," Georgia mumbled. She buried her face back in her book, uninterested by what was transpiring.

"Oh, just think of him marrying one of you girls," their mother sighed. "How happy that should make your father and I."

Georgia turned the page, knowing full well that what her mother meant by 'marrying one of you girls' she meant marrying Evangelina.

She knew that because Georgia Hamilton was not pretty. At least, she was not considered pretty in the traditional sense. Her sister, however, was considered to be the beauty of the country. Where Georgia's dark hair lacked luster, Evangelina's lighter features gleamed. Where Georgia's pale, thin lips opened up to a pleasant smile, Evangelina's full, red ones revealed a smile that brightened the room. Where Georgia's figure was, well, fuller, Evangelina's was slender and elegant.

These, of course, were all of the comparisons that Georgia had lived with since she could remember. Her sister was the beautiful one; while she was the eldest one. This had long stopped bothering Georgia, however. She learned to ignore the small comparisons people whispered about her and her sister. She had already acknowledged that she was on the plain side, and, therefore, not destined for great things ,and at nearly twenty-three, she was well on her way to spinsterhood.

"Oh, mother, I must have a new dress," Evangelina exclaimed. "I have already worn all the other ones."

"Yes, yes, of course, my dear," her mother replied. "I will not have you seen in something you have worn already. We shall all have new dresses."

"Well, perhaps not Georgia," Evangelina laughed. "She would much prefer a book."

"I would," Georgia agreed tonelessly not even looking up.

Evangelina huffed. "How strange you are."

"How silly *you* are," Georgia blandly retorted as she turned another page.

Her sister scoffed.

"That is enough, girls," Mrs. Hamilton warned. "You will give me a headache." She squeezed the bridge of her nose with her thumb and forefinger. "Georgia, go and order us some tea, please."

Evangelina smirked at her sister triumphantly as Georgia obediently put down her book and rose from the couch slightly annoyed but glad for the excuse to leave the room. She had been long used to her mother and sister ganging up on her. As she made her way out the hall, she saw one of their servants dusting and decided to give the task to her.

"Martha, could you have some tea sent to Mrs. Hamilton and Miss Evangelina, please?"

Martha curtseyed. "Yes, ma'am," she replied leaving her dusting and making her way to the kitchen.

Georgia decided to see what her father was up to, so moved to the other side of the house where his study was located. She knocked lightly on the doorframe the door having already been open.

Her father, not expecting the intrusion, jumped slightly, his face riddled in an expression Georgia couldn't recall ever seeing him make before.

She frowned. "Did I scare you, papa?" she asked.

He quickly put a smile on his face. "Not at all, child," he replied holding out his hand and inviting her in.

Georgia smiled in return and moved to her father's side to give him a kiss on the cheek. "What are reading?" she asked him innocently. "Is it a letter from uncle?"

Her father folded the piece of paper up and stuffed it under a book. "It is a letter of business, I am afraid," he told her. "Something I would never bother you with."

Georgia creased her brow and tilted her head slightly. "I would not mind if you did," she replied. "You have never shied away from sharing business letters with me before."

He patted her hand. "Yes, but some business is not meant for young ladies, my dear," her father said as he seemingly forced a smile.

Georgia regarded her father for a moment. "Very well," she sighed. "I suppose I would have found it odious and boring."

"Indeed, you would have."

There was a brief silence between them.

"What are your mother and sister up to then? Scheming no doubt?"

Georgia grinned. "What else?" she replied. "Mother received word about a prestigious visitor the Dorsets will be welcoming soon."

"A rich, single man?" her father guessed.

"Is there any other kind of visitor?" She smirked. "He is their nephew, apparently, and is to be present at their ball next week."

"And what do we think of him so far?" her father teased. "Are you already madly in love with this rich, single young man?"

"More than I could dare to dream!" Georgia replied in an exaggerated manner.

Her father chuckled.

"I am sure he is only handsome because his money makes him so," Georgia said in a more serious manner. "If he had a wort on his nose and teeth like a rat, I am sure everyone would be willing to look past it with eight thousand a year."

"Eight thousand a year, did you say?" her father repeated almost breathlessly, his interest piqued.

Georgia laughed at her father. "Not you, too!" she exclaimed. "There has to be someone other than myself who does not lose her mind over a man's large income."

"Eight thousand a year would be a wonderful thing for you girls," he told her. "How fine you both would be."

Georgia laughed. "Are we not fine now, papa? Your income is not so small! I am sure you made plenty of women swoon at the sound of it when you were younger."

Her father smiled, though fleetingly. "Yes, I perhaps might have. But eight thousand a year is a fine prospect for you."

Georgia frowned. "You mean for Evangelina," she corrected. "A man with eight thousand a year, papa, is not going to look twice at me but to point out a blemish on my face."

Her father looked at her somberly. "My dear Georgia," he started, "do you not know there is more to give a man than a pretty face?"

Georgia shrugged a little indifferently. "What difference would it make either way?" she asked. "What am I to do with eight thousand a year? It is not like we need it."

He nodded slowly. "Come," he told her after a moment. "Let us join your mother and sister for tea. I am sure their conversation is lacking sense."

She gave a weak smile, but nodded and followed her father out of the room.

2

For the next week, the only thing Georgia's mother and sister could talk about were the prospects of the ball. Dresses and hairstyles and dance partners were the only topics the two women seemed to care about. Even her father would join in every so often. It was enough to drive anyone mad.

Georgia, therefore, to avoid it all spent her time reading outdoors or going for walks around the neighborhood. She had hoped that she could spend the evening of the ball alone, at home, but when the time came, she was surprised that she was expected to go.

"I do not understand," she almost argued. "I have never been made to go to a ball before if I did not want to. What is so different about this one?"

"Georgia, there will no quarreling over this," her father replied gently. "We were invited as a family and as a family we will go."

Thus, Georgia found herself at the Dorset's ball, thrown among the extravagance and splendor she had wanted no part in. Silently she made her way to the opposite side of the dancefloor where she was greeted by her friend Ross Fairgrove.

He smiled and gave her a slight bow.

"Have you finished your studies already, Ross?" she asked him. "I thought classes did not end until next week?"

He shook his head. "I got back a few days ago," he replied. "Classes have been over for over a week now."

"And you are finished for good?"

He sighed softly. "For good."

"I congratulate you," she said beaming at her friend. "It is a great accomplishment."

He thanked her heartily.

"What are you to do now? Are you to join your uncle in the law?"

Ross bobbed his head. "It has been talked of, but I am yet undecided."

"What would you do otherwise?" she asked, but he didn't hear her, and she watched as his eyes lit up when her sister came into view.

"Miss Evangelina," he said with a bow.

Evangelina shot him a quick glance. "Mr. Fairgrove," she replied in a partially strained voice before turning her attention to her sister. "Have you seen Jennifer and Jessica?"

Georgia felt shame for her sister at her mistreatment of Ross but said nothing on the point. Instead, she answered her sister's question and pointed in the direction she saw the two Hayes sisters.

"Miss Evangelina," Ross Fairgrove choked out as she moved away. "Might you honor me with a dance later this evening?"

"I will think about it," Evangelina replied without looking back, leaving Ross deflated.

Ross Fairgrove had been connected to the Hamilton family since he and Georgia were children. He was from a respectable family with a modest, decent income. He was intelligent, kind, thoughtful, and had been hopelessly in love with Evangelina since she was fifteen years old. However much he felt for her, Evangelina seemed to care almost nothing for him. Though he was not frightful to look at, his average features did not seem to inspire anything more than boredom and apathy within her.

Georgia smiled at him sympathetically. "She does not mean anything by it," she told him.

"Do you think me a fool for trying?" Ross asked her.

"Yes," Georgia replied bluntly, never having a reason for letting someone down gently. "You go through the same cycle every time."

"I know," he sighed. "I just keep hoping that today will be the day that she finally says, 'yes.'"

"Though it is very strange," Georgia mused. "It was not long ago that the two of you were rather close. I had at one time thought—" she stopped herself. She was going to say that she once thought her sister in love with him, but had decided better of it. What good would it have done to wound her friend more?

Ross nodded. "Perhaps, we were. Or," he paused, "perhaps we were both mistaken."

There was a strange hush over the other guests and Georgia turned to see what was the cause. Everyone had stopped their conversations to look at the young man that had just entered the ballroom.

"Who is that?" Georgia asked. "And why is everyone making such a big fuss over him?"

"That is Mr. Garrett," Ross explained. "He is the Dorsets' nephew. All the women here will be throwing themselves at him no doubt."

"Yes, including my sister," Georgia added, regretting her comment as soon as she said it.

Ross gave a strained smile.

She sighed. "I do wish Louisa were here. At least she would laugh at this scene with me. Have you heard from her recently?"

"My sister and her husband are both well," he informed her. "My mother has just returned from a short stay with them."

"I am glad to hear it. I have not heard from her lately and I was beginning to worry."

"Do not look, but here he comes now."

"Who?" Georgia turned to see Mr. Garrett walking in their direction.

"Why would you look if I asked you not to?" Ross whispered harshly.

"That is the exact thing people do when you tell them not to do things," she replied in the same tone. "They do that exact thing."

"Mr. Fairgrove," Mr. Garrett said in a pleasant, melodic voice—a pure voice. It was the only voice that could have come from someone as handsome as the man before them. His prominent cheek bones, his sparkling green eyes blinking under impossibly perfect lashes that seemed to flutter as his full, red lips revealed a dazzling smile. All of that was complete with raven black hair that bounced almost imperceptibly as he spoke; the soft timbre of his voice having the ability to melt away the coldest of winters.

Yes, he was handsome and the ridiculousness of how much his handsome features and voice matched each other overcame Georgia causing her to look away to stifle a laugh.

"Mr. Garret, it is nice to see you again," Ross replied.

The men bowed at each other, though one more elegantly and perfectly than the other.

"I was very glad to see a face I recognized," Mr. Garrett told him. "I did not expect my aunt and uncle to invite the whole county. I feel as if I am in a sea of strangers."

Georgia felt for him, realizing, that despite his good looks and fortune being the best kind of recommendations, he was rather shy.

"Well, I do hope you can swim then because sooner or later I do believe the tide will come in and whisk you away," Georgia replied playfully, nodding to the less than obvious onlookers.

Mr. Garrett smiled softly at her. "I am sure it will," he replied.

"Forgive me," Ross started. "Mr. Garrett, this is Miss Georgia Hamilton. Miss Hamilton, this is Mr. Garrett."

"It is a pleasure to meet you, Miss Hamilton," Mr. Garrett told her with a bow.

"The pleasure is all mine. It is nice to put a face to the man the whole county has been talking about," she teased.

Mr. Garrett coughed and, perhaps, blushed. "Am I so famous already?" he shyly joked.

"Word spreads fast out in the country," she told him. "But do not fret. Most of the people here are harmless. If you are to fear anyone, however, it would be the scheming mothers to unattached daughters."

To this Mr. Garrett chuckled. "I believe that is the fear of most men in my situation," he replied. "Thank you for your advice. I shall certainly heed it."

Mr. Garrett was then called away by his aunt and his long evening of introductions began.

"You were flirting with him," Ross pointed out.

"What?" Georgia said.

"With Mr. Garrett just now. You were flirting."

"I was not flirting," Georgia laughed. "The poor man obviously cannot go anywhere without the weight of very high expectations of everyone around him on his shoulders. I was just trying to make him feel more comfortable."

Ross huffed. "You do not have to hide yourself from me, Georgia Hamilton," he said. "I have known you for too long."

"Is that so?"

"Yes, and I know that deep down under your façade of stoic demeanor, lies the heart of a true romantic."

She lifted a brow at her friend. "Do not be ridiculous, Ross," she replied. "I am allowed to be kind."

"Especially if that kindness is directed at a very handsome and rich young man?" he challenged in a harsh tone.

"What kind of mood is this?" she asked him. "Why are you being so irritable today?"

He shook his head. "Never mind. Forgive me. I have been of a brooding nature lately."

"Well, stop it, or else I will not want to be around you," Georgia told him.

He nodded. "Forgive me. I have had a lot on my mind as of late."

"Well, put your mind at ease for a few hours and escort me to dinner," she gently ordered as the bell rang. "Then, later, I expect you to dance with me at least once and you better have a smile on your face by then."

Ross laughed through his nose. "I shall try."

Dancing began soon after dinner with men quickly claiming their prospective partners. Ross without even asking, since he had practically been ordered, led Georgia onto the dance floor for the first set.

Both of their eyes wandered about the floor, watching and

observing the other couples as they danced. Ross frowned when he saw Evangelina smiling across the line at her partner. Georgia noticed his expression and followed his glaring eyes to a man she might have seen once before.

"Who is he?" Georgia asked him as the dance began.

"Who?" Ross replied, half distracted.

"The man dancing with my sister."

Ross huffed. "That is Vince Talbot. I believe he is a distant relative of one of the late king's bastards. Though I am sure he is a bastard himself."

"Ross," Georgia half laughed. "I thought I scolded you out of this mood earlier."

"I am out of sorts, I know," he replied. "I do not feel myself today."

"Are you unwell? Perhaps you should go home?"

He nodded. "Perhaps I should."

"You would leave me here all alone to wade through the masses as they drool over the illustriously handsome Mr. Garret?"

Ross smirked, though fleetingly. "I thought you found my mood abhorrent?"

"I do, but if I am to spend the evening here alone, I might go mad."

"More than the masses?" he asked, raising a brow. "At least the scene could give you something to write about. It has been a while since I have had the pleasure of one of your stories."

Georgia smiled, gratified, but shook her head. "It has been a while since I have felt the urge to write. I have hit a dry spell as of late."

"Well, please let me know when the talented Lady H has another book in need of publishing."

Georgia blushed at the sound of her pen name. "Hush! You will be overheard," she whispered.

He shook his head. "No one here has any idea of what we speak. That reminds me. I do have a few more royalties for you."

Georgia's eyes grew wide. "Do you?"

"Eight pounds this month alone for *The Winds of Westbrook*. Your publisher is pleased."

"Eight pounds," Georgia repeated.

Ross nodded as his gaze drifted back to Evangelina.

"Ow!" Georgia cried out. "You stood on my foot!"

Ross started, his cheeks flushing with embarrassment. "Forgive me, Georgia, I was distracted." He huffed. "Last month it was Mr. Barger, and a few months before him, she had Mr. Fields in her sights. And not long before that, it was me." He shook her head. "I wonder who will be her next conquest after she leaves him in the wind?"

Georgia nodded, pitying her friend knowing how much of a flirt her sister could be and Mr. Talbot appeared to be her new favorite.

"She is still young, Ross. I am sure, like a lot of young girls her age with beauty on her side, she is just exercising her powers over the opposite sex. She will tire of it in a year or two. I am sure of it."

He clenched his teeth and nodded. "I am sure."

When the dance was finally over, Ross complained of a headache and went home leaving Georgia without a partner for several dances. She fell into conversation here and there with some of the other guests, but soon found herself alone. Her feet aching and tired, she sat herself on a chair along the wall where she had a perfect view of the dance floor. She smiled as she watched the couples float about the floor studying the expressions on their faces.

The eyes of the younger women—those yet to be married—had hope shining in them as they gazed upon their handsome partners. The men—married or otherwise—seemed to hope for something more than just a dance.

"Why is it you are not dancing?" came a cool voice, pulling her from her observations.

Georgia looked up and saw the much-anticipated Adam Garrett taking a seat next to her. He seemed more handsome in the ballroom lighting. She smiled softly as she took in his sculpted features, the candlelight dancing in his eyes. She couldn't help but admire his looks. She even appreciated the way his dark hair curled ever so slightly.

"Well," she began folding her hands in her lap, "it would appear I am not dancing because no one has asked, and I assumed it would look rather silly me dancing a reel by myself."

"Do imaginary partners not count?" he teased back with a raised brow.

Georgia laughed. "Not in some circles, but I suppose an imaginary partner is all some can hope for."

"How do you mean?" he asked, his brow slightly creased.

She shrugged slightly. "Never mind me," she told him. "I am a bitter sort."

"You seem too young to be bitter," he replied standing only to take two glasses of champagne from a servant passing by. He handed her one.

She thanked him, taking the proffered glass. "I sometimes doubt whether bitterness has anything to do with age, but comes more with experience," she explained.

"Does not experience come with age?" he philosophized back.

She grinned. "Does not one person's experience differ from another's? Cannot one person experience more than another in the same amount of time?"

"For example?" He took a sip of his champagne.

Georgia inhaled slightly and let it out in a huff as she thought. "Does not a soldier in the field of battle experience more than a man of the same age and background who does nothing but sit at home all day?"

Mr. Garrett nodded. "I see your point. How right you are." He lifted his glass to her. "To the young and bitter."

She raised her glass as well and took a sip from it. "Why are you not dancing, Mr. Garrett?" she asked after a moment.

"I supposed it is because I have not asked anyone," he replied with a shrug.

"Ah, I see. What a conundrum."

Mr. Garrett grinned and laughed through his nose.

Georgia liked the look of his face as he did so. She quickly looked away, realizing she might have been staring for too long.

"Would it offend your imaginary partner if I asked *you* to dance?"

Georgia stifled a laugh. "I am not sure. He is certainly of the jealous type."

"Would you care to chance it?"

Georgia was taken aback. At first, she had thought he was only joining in on her playful banter, but looking at him, she realized he was being quite serious.

"That is very kind of you to ask," she replied cautiously. "Do you not have other ladies waiting in your wake for a turn?"

He shrugged. "I suppose my aunt has a list of women for me somewhere, but I have been justifiably avoiding her."

Georgia laughed, surprised by his answer.

"The next set will be starting soon," he pointed out. "And you have not answered."

"Oh!" she exclaimed. "Yes, I will dance with you!"

"I am relieved. I thought for a moment you might reject me!"

"A disappointment I am sure you rarely experience."

He frowned at her. "Why would you think that?"

Georgia shook her head. "I am only teasing. Forgive me, you are not used to my humor. My mother often tells me that I am not serious enough when I ought to be, and too serious when I ought not."

He grinned, amused. "A bit of a rebel, I suppose?"

"The worst kind."

"Mr. Garrett, is silly Georgia Hamilton distressing you with her stern demeanor and bitter conversations?" came the less-than-pleasant voice of Veronica Lewis, a girl of high means and little brains.

Georgia averted her eyes, half embarrassed, half annoyed that someone as dull as Veronica Lewis would talk about her in such a way.

"Not at all, Miss Lewis," Mr. Garrett replied. "I was actually enjoying our conversation. I have yet to be so amused this evening. Miss Hamilton certainly has an interesting view on things."

Georgia felt her stomach twist in knots while Veronica gaped at him.

"Come, Miss Hamilton," Mr. Garrett said as he stood, offering her his hand. "I believe the next dance is about to start."

Georgia didn't hesitate as she took his hand and allowed him to lead her to the dance floor. Several people stared and even more whispered as Georgia stood across from Mr. Garrett. It was almost unfathomable to the people of Barchester that a girl as plain as Georgia could ever stand up with a man as handsome as Mr. Garrett. Georgia was the sad version of an unfished work of art, while Mr. Garrett was the Sistine chapel itself. What could it mean?

"I believe everyone is looking at us," Mr. Garrett said as they danced.

"I am sure they are," Georgia replied. "I am sure they stared at you and the other girls you danced with earlier in the evening as well. They are curious as to whom you look best with."

He smiled. "Yet, I have not danced with anyone else," he told her. "You are the first one I have asked."

Georgia felt herself blush and her skin prickle. "I am the first person you have danced with this evening?"

He nodded singularly. "Yes. I have not danced with anyone else."

Georgia was not sure how to reply, so didn't.

He cleared his throat. "The young woman a few people down is your sister, is she not?" He gestured with his head.

Georgia looked over at her sister dancing with the same man from earlier. "Yes, that is Evangelina. I can introduce you to her if you would like," Georgia suggested, her heart dropping, knowing that he probably would.

"We have already been introduced," he replied.

"You should ask her to dance then," Georgia urged. "She is full of energy and good humor." She frowned, unsure as to why she was lying about her sister's 'good' qualities to this man.

He nodded. "I guess it is expected of me to ask more than one woman to dance."

Mr. Garrett bowed when the dance was over and escorted Georgia to get a drink where her sister was talking to Vince Talbot. Georgia watched her sister closely for a moment before observing Mr. Talbot. She did not like how closely he was standing next to her.

"Lina," she said, bringing her sister's attention to her for a moment.

"Georgie." She smirked. "Did I see you dancing just now?"

"She is a rather pleasant partner," Mr. Garrett answered for her. "Your sister is an accomplished dancer."

At this, Evangelina looked a little surprised. "Is she?" she replied. "Strange. I have never heard her described as such before. She very rarely dances."

"Just because you have not heard it, does not make it untrue," Mr. Garrett said in reply.

Evangelina smiled playfully at this. "Are you free for the next dance, Mr. Garrett?" she boldly asked. "Mr. Talbot here has already declared he is done with dancing and now I am left without a partner."

Mr. Talbot scoffed.

Mr. Garrett looked from Georgia to Evangelina. "If your sister does not mind."

"Oh, Georgia never minds," Evangelina told him. "As I said before, she rarely dances."

"It is true," Georgia replied softly. "I much prefer conversation."

"See?" Evangelina said. "She is well, and you are free to dance with me."

Mr. Garrett bowed shallowly before he led Evangelina, who sneered triumphantly at Mr. Talbot, to the dance floor. Mr. Talbot then walked to the other side of the room in what Georgia thought was a rather angry pace.

Satisfied that her sister was dancing with someone other than Mr. Talbot and that she would not be the only person with whom Mr.

Garrett asked to dance, Georgia made her way out of the ballroom and down the hall to look for her father. As she was about to turn the corner into another room she stopped, hearing her name being uttered in conversation.

"Did you see Georgia Hamilton standing up with Mr. Garrett?" came the hushed voice of one of the Hayes twins.

"Is he not a dream?" replied the other one just as softly.

"He must have the kindest disposition," she heard the first girl whisper in response.

"Yes!" the other girl agreed. "How else would you explain him dancing with her? It must have been out of pity seeing she was sitting alone."

"Oh, that handsome man! Watching him dance with her did anger me at first, but you are right, he must have done it out of kindness. For he could never care for her."

Georgia repressed the twinge of anger and pain welling inside of her and forced a smile on her face as she walked into the room. She beamed at the twins, their identical appearance still unsettling to her even though she had known them since they were both little girls.

"Good evening, Jennifer, Jessica," she said to them.

The two sisters looked uncomfortable, as if they feared she might have overheard them talking about her.

"Have you seen my father?" she asked.

The twins slowly turned their heads to glance at one another before looking back at Georgia who shivered as their eyes met.

"No," they both said in unison.

Georgia nodded curtly. "Thank you anyway."

She turned and left the room hoping to soon find her father and tell him that she had long since been ready to return home. She rounded another corner and found him talking to the host, Mr. Dorset.

"Ah, Miss Hamilton!" Mr. Dorset said with a smile when he saw her. "I see my nephew asked you to dance. He is a kind fellow, is he not?"

Georgia forced a smile. "Yes, very kind. He saw I was without a partner and took responsibility as any gentleman should," she replied.

"Yes, he never wishes to see anyone left out," Mr. Dorset continued. "Good man." He waved at another guest and excused himself as he moved to talk to them.

"Is everything alright, my dear?" her father asked seeing she was a little put out by Mr. Dorset's presumptuous comment about his nephew dancing with her.

"Yes," she replied with a façade of happiness. "I think I am just overtired."

Her father nodded. "I am glad to hear it. I have been looking for an excuse to leave for the past hour," he told her. "Having not been to one of these events in so long, I have forgotten how much I abhor them."

Georgia laughed quietly.

"Come, we shall find your mother and sister," he said extending his arm for her to take.

"What? Leave now?" Mrs. Hamilton complained when they found her happily watching her *pretty* daughter flirt with Mr. Garrett. "We cannot possibly go! Look at how Mr. Garrett is warming up to Evangelina. If we leave now, another woman could take her place in his affections."

"If you are so certain of his fickleness, mamma, why would you want your daughter associated with him at all?" Georgia asked, watching her sister flutter about Mr. Garrett, who blushed and smiled in return.

"Oh, hush, child," her mother scolded. "What would you know of it?"

"That is enough, my dear," Mr. Hamilton said sternly. "I am tired and wish to be surrounded by the comforts of my own home."

"But, Mr. Hamilton—"

"Georgia, go and tell your sister we are leaving," her father directed her. "I shall have the carriage ordered."

Georgia nodded and left her mother's disappointment to pull her sister away from the man everyone had such high hopes for. He gave a half bow as she approached.

"Miss Hamilton," he said in greeting. "I had wondered where you gone, I was hoping—"

"I am sure she was perusing the books in your aunt and uncle's library," Evangelina interjected. "She is often in search of her next read."

"You are an avid reader, then?" he asked her, his eyes lighting up.

Georgia smiled politely. "I do not know about avid, but I love to read, yes."

"Perhaps we read the same. What are your favorites?" Mr. Garrett asked her.

Georgia opened her mouth to reply when her sister interrupted.

"Oh, we cannot discuss books while we are at a ball!" Evangelina proclaimed. "Balls are meant for dancing and for love making; it is not for books."

"Yes, and it is also for getting to know new acquaintances," Georgia added with a sly look at Mr. Garrett. "And one cannot fully know someone without understanding what he or she likes to read."

"I agree with you," Mr. Garrett said. "Knowing how one perceives a book allows you into their mind. It is a key into the depths of their soul."

Evangelina gaped at him, while Georgia smiled.

"That was very poetic," she said. "And as much as I like a good philosophical conversation, I am afraid I came over here with the sole purpose of taking my sister away."

"What?" Evangelina said.

"Papa wishes to be home," Georgia explained.

"Go home now?" Evangelina shot back. "It is still early. It is only just past midnight. Could papa not wait another couple hours? I am sure I have not had my fill of dancing."

"It is out of my hands," she told her sister. "He has already ordered the carriage."

Evangelina sighed elegantly. "Well, I guess, that decides it."

"Come, we must find the hosts and bid them goodnight." Georgia turned to Mr. Garrett. "Mr. Garrett, thank you for an evening of pleasant conversation. It was a pleasure to meet you."

Mr. Garrett bowed again. "The pleasure was all mine," he replied. "I hope to visit with you soon, if I may?"

"Of course, you will always be welcome at our home," Evangelina replied giving him one of her charming smiles and curtseying.

The two girls looped arms as they walked away, one still pining over the dancing she was being denied, the other ignoring her sister's complaints.

Mr. Garrett watched them both as they went with a strange sense of intrigue as he did so.

3

The whole town was buzzing about the ball the next day, throwing Mr. Garrett's name around to anyone who would listen. Everyone was delighted with his manners, his handsome looks, his excessive income! Though it was regrettable he did not dance more, who he danced with was much talked about.

Everyone was quite shocked to see Mr. Garrett stand up with Georgia Hamilton. It was almost unnatural to see a man as good looking as him dancing with a woman as plain as the dead leaves that littered the forest floor, but after his second choice, it was understood.

Evangelina, who had inherited all of the beauty in the family, was obviously the reason he danced with Georgia. It was agreed that he asked Georgia, the sister with little consequence to anyone, as a means to get into the good graces of her sister. Through Georgia, therefore, he was able to ask the much prettier Miss Hamilton to dance.

After half the town discussed this over the course of a few days, it was decided that Mr. Garrett, who asked no one to dance after the Hamiltons had left, was half in love with Evangelina already. Now, the only thing left to do was to bet on how long it would take for Mr. Garrett to propose.

THE MAIL HAD COME LATE THAT MORNING, AND, SINCE IT HAD NOT arrived at the usual time, no one was expecting anything. However, as Georgia was just about to get ready for a walk, a servant surprised her with a letter written in a hand she knew all too well. Her breath caught when she saw it and a slight blush creeped onto her cheeks as she calmly took it from the servant.

Fearing prying eyes she saved her letter until she got to the large, towering oak tree past the gardens. She sat on the bench under its shade and broke the seal to the letter.

My dearest Georgia,

It has been a fortnight since I have received your last letter, and I am ashamed I have let so much time pass before I answered it. I hope you have not forgotten me until now, though I would not blame you if my neglectfulness has thrown you into the arms of another man.

Apologies aside, I have been rather busy traveling and visiting my sister in London. I shall be staying here for a couple of months at the attached address and hope to pay more attention to our correspondence. I truly miss your letters. Your poetic way with words and beautifully mentioned sentiments makes our separation more bearable.

I promise I shall write again soon.

William

Georgia pressed her hand to her hot cheek. She had not heard from William in several weeks and was beginning to worry something had happened but holding his letter in her hand relieved her of any such anxiety.

She delayed her walk and returned to the house to reply, giddy with excitement. It was the same way she felt every time she received one of his letters. It had been nearly a year now since they first began their correspondence and Georgia often reread his letters when a new one couldn't be had. It was the first one, however, that she had read the most.

"*Dear Miss Georgia Hamilton,*" the letter had begun. "*I do not know if you will remember me, but I assure you that I have not stopped thinking of you since the day we met this past summer.*"

Georgia's cheeks had flushed crimson when she first received it and she had to read the sentence two more times to make sure she had not mistaken what it said.

"*We met several occasions at my cousins' the Stanfords and since the moment I saw you, I have never met a woman worth knowing more than you. Your beauty is more than just your physical features, but a deep understanding of the world.*

"I cannot tell you how many times I have agonized over writing to you, and I must confess I have started many letters only to throw them away soon after starting them. How could I convey the depth of my feeling for you in words that could make you understand the impact our brief acquaintance has had on me? How could I explain my torment, or agony without you thinking me mad?

"But at last, I have settled on this letter in the hopes that you would return a few lines to me. I shall not dare dream you could feel the same as I do for you, no, but I shall wish, if it is to your liking, to correspond with you for a time. I have hopes of returning to Barchester again perhaps next summer and of seeing you."

"Yours in affectionate hope, William Henry."

Georgia had been stunned. Of course, she remembered William Henry. She had met him and spoken with him on multiple occasions during his stay here, but she could not recall there being any indication that he had felt anything for her. At times, she did not even think he had looked at her.

Was it just because he was shy and unable to do so? Could he truly feel for her?

Georgia had read the letter again and then a third time. Should she respond immediately? In a few days? Should she reply at all? Certainly, this was not for her. Such were the thoughts that ran through her head. After a lifetime of never being told she was pretty or desired, it was something she realized she *had* desired.

Her stomach had churned as she stopped and read the letter a fourth time just to make sure it said what it had said. To her relief, the words had not changed. They had remained constant, faithful to her and her feelings.

She nodded as she decided. She would write immediately but would not post it for a day or two. Or would she post it immediately?

Once in her room, she had pulled the letter back out and read it a fifth time. She sighed once she finished, her heart fluttering strangely. She had never heard such beautiful words directed toward her before.

Could they truly be real?

Georgia had paced her room for several more minutes before she read the letter yet again. She pressed the creased paper against her heart and sighed. After a moment, she folded it and threw it on her vanity.

No!

What a beautiful farce this letter was.

She had sat down on her bed and stared at the piece of paper from across the room. She scrutinized over it; its words; its meaning; the handwriting it was written in. Then, after mulling it over in her mind for half an hour, she decided to do what she already decided an hour before.

She was going to respond.

Determined, Georgia stood from her bed and marched to her writing desk. She pulled out a fresh sheet of paper and dipped her quill into the ink. She hesitated, the tip of the quill hovering over the paper.

After taking a deep breath, she began. Her quill scratched against the paper in a fury of words and just as she was about to sign off on what she had written, she balled it up and threw it into the corner of the room.

She had pulled out another piece of paper and began the same process a few more times, dissatisfied with every attempt to convey a message that was not only intelligible, but encouraging.

Finally, after the fifth attempt, she had settled on a few short lines.

Dear Mr. Henry,

I must say I was quite shocked by your letter. I had not realized during our short acquaintance you felt that way. This does not go to say your letter was unwelcome. It was rather a pleasant surprise.

I remember our time together during your stay rather fondly and would enjoy continuing a correspondence with you. I hope you are well and wish to hear from you soon.

Georgia Hamilton.

Georgia had stared at her fifth draft. She had not altogether been pleased with it but could not think of anything else to add. Therefore, she was determined to be satisfied. Besides, she did not have all day to write a silly love letter.

She had caught herself at this. A *love letter*, she had thought. A *love letter was sent to me!*

That had been almost a year ago and since then, she and William had continuously been writing to one another. Almost one letter a week passed between them, and it had been a joy that Georgia had never known before.

As she was making her way back to the house, she was blessed by another surprise; Mr. Garrett was just dismounting his horse. Georgia quickly folded her letter and hid it in her pocket.

"Mr. Garrett," she said with a curtsey. "How are you?"

He bowed. "I am well, thank you. Are you just coming back from a walk?"

"Yes," Georgia replied. "I often do around this time, weather permitting, of course."

"Naturally."

"Would you like to come in?" she asked him, gesturing toward the house. "I am sure my sister is in the back parlor."

He looked confused and opened his mouth to respond but nodded instead.

"Have you been enjoying your time here in Barchester so far?" she asked as she led him into the house.

"Yes, it is very beautiful here," he replied.

"Is it very different from—I am so sorry. I do not know where you are from," Georgia apologized.

He smiled. "Cornwall."

She raised her brows. "Really?" she replied. "Are you into mining?"

"My family has stakes in a couple of mines, but our main business is in the transportation and selling of the loads."

"For your sake, I am glad for it," Georgia told him.

"Why is that?"

"Mining is such an unstable and unpredictable business. One day, they are producing a fortune's worth of material, the next they are closed because everything worth mining has already been depleted."

He looked at her in pleasant surprise. "I agree."

She smiled at him as she opened the parlor door. "Mamma, Evangelina, Mr. Garrett has come to pay us a visit," she announced as she showed him in.

Mrs. Hamilton stood gracefully though a little flustered by the surprise. "Oh, Mr. Garrett, what a pleasure to see you again so soon. Come, come, we were just about to order tea."

"Good afternoon, Mr. Garrett," Evangelina said with a smile.

Mr. Garrett bowed and returned the greeting. "I hope I have not come at an inconvenient time."

"Of course, you have not," Mrs. Hamilton reassured him. "We were all rather bored with the day. I am glad you have come to liven it up."

"I do apologize that we left rather suddenly the other night," Evangelina told him. "Poor papa had come down with a headache. That is why he urged us away so early."

"I hope he is not unwell," Mr. Garrett inquired.

"Right as rain. Thank you for asking," Mrs. Hamilton replied. "A good sleep does one well."

Mr. Garrett nodded. "I couldn't agree more."

Having nothing to add to this forced, unintelligible conversation, Georgia decided to excuse herself.

"You will not stay for tea?" Mr. Garrett asked as she moved to the door.

Georgia looked at her sister and mother, and, seeing as she was not needed by them, replied in the negative. "Forgive me, but I have a letter to write. I have neglected the correspondence between myself and a friend for too long." She curtseyed and hurried away, leaving Mr. Garrett to her mother and Evangelina's devices.

After an hour's perusal of old letters, Georgia reread her own. She smiled down at it.

My dear William,

I must confess, I was beginning to worry that you had forgotten about me. But I have forgiven you for your neglect! Family is important and I long to hear of your adventures with your nephews.

She went on to tell him about the ball and the new arrival of Mr. Garrett causing a fuss in the neighborhood.

I do wish you would return so that we might stand up together at the next gathering.

She blushed at this. It was a bold statement, but she meant it, and she was not one to back down from what she felt.

After she finished perusing the letter, she folded it neatly and rang the bell for a servant to take the letter for posting. She then put a triumphant smile on her face and marched downstairs.

She poked her head into her father's office and saw that he was writing a letter of his own.

"Has uncle replied yet about letting Margot come to London with us this year?" she asked him.

Her father looked up at her, rather confused at being knocked from his thoughts. "What is that, child?" he asked her.

"Is cousin Margot going to come to London with us this year?" she repeated.

He shook his head. "I have not gone over the details with my brother yet," he told her.

Georgia studied her father for a moment; he seemed tired and worn out as if something was weighing on his mind. "Papa, is everything alright?" she asked cautiously.

He sighed a little more exasperatedly than he wanted to and smiled. "I am well, child," he said after a moment. "I am just getting older quicker than I planned to."

Georgia grinned and laughed through her nose. "I am sure we all do, papa," she added. "But are you sure there is nothing else? You have seemed," she paused, "a little out of sorts as of late."

"Yes, yes, I am well," he reassured her. "I have no concerns with my health."

"Then, is it something else that has been bothering you?"

He eyed his eldest daughter for a moment. "Are you so sure something is?"

Georgia hesitated in her response. "Perhaps, not." She gave her father a kiss on his forehead. "I shall have some tea ordered for us," she told him. "Mamma and Evangelina have already had theirs with Mr. Garrett."

"Did they?" he said in surprise. "I did not know he had come."

She nodded. "I escorted him in myself."

"Then we are saved," he mumbled under his breath.

"What is that, papa?"

Her father shook his head. "Nothing! Nothing! Never you mind, child," he gesticulated. "Order us some fine tea. We can enjoy it while you tell me all about the latest book you have read. Or about the one you have yet to write."

Georgia grinned. "I shall be right back."

He watched his daughter leave the study and relaxed back into his chair. "We are saved," he whispered to himself. "God, let us be saved."

4

Georgia was excited, when a few days later, she received another letter. She was slightly disappointed, however, as the letter was not from William Henry, but from her most intimate friend Louisa Barker. She felt rather ashamed and silly that she should be disappointed, especially when she had not heard from her friend in over a month. But the feelings that the letters from Mr. Henry inspired in her were so different from anything that she ever experienced; she had hoped that a response would come sooner rather than later.

She quickly scolded herself for these feelings, knowing full well that her letter had most likely not even arrived at its destination yet. Recollecting herself, she sighed and smiled as she happily opened the letter from her friend. Her happiness only grew when she realized the letter was an invitation to come and visit.

Whatever minute disappointment she felt upon receiving the letter, soon after melted away as the hopes of seeing her friend filled her thoughts. Louisa, having greatly missed her, wished she could come in a few months' time to "stay for no less than six weeks."

Elated, Georgia hurriedly sought out her father's permission, who readily agreed.

"What a capitol idea," he told her. "I am sure Louisa would love seeing you and it would most likely give her a much-needed break from her husband."

Georgia laughed. "Papa, you are wicked."

"Once you are married, my dear, you will understand."

Georgia's smile faded slightly. "I am sure I will," she replied quietly, hoping but not yet believing she would ever get the chance to understand.

At any rate, she quickly wrote her reply and acquiescence. On her way to hand it to a servant for posting, she was met by Mr. Garrett who was just being let in by the butler.

He bowed. "Miss Hamilton, it is a pleasure to see you again."

She smiled, readjusting her glasses. "Likewise, though I must tell you my sister is not in today. She is visiting the Hayes."

He blinked, his nose wrinkled as he laughed quietly. "Is there any reason I cannot visit with you?" he asked.

Georgia shook her head at the innocent question, chuckling at the way Mr. Garrett's expression brightened his eyes. "There is not. I am quite free." She then handed the butler her letter, asking him to post it.

"I have borrowed my uncle's phaeton," he told her. "Would you care to go for a ride with me? I have not yet been very far in the neighborhood and was hoping for a bit of a tour."

Mrs. Hamilton happened to walk out into the hall at that moment. She greeted Mr. Garrett with a sincere though reserved demeanor.

"I did not know you had come, Mr. Garret," she told him. "How very good to see you again."

"Yes, I felt so welcomed the last time I came," he said.

Georgia thought she saw her mother blush. "He is wanting to go on a tour of the neighborhood," she interjected. "He has borrowed his uncle's phaeton just for the occasion."

"That is a splendid idea," her mother said. "I am sorry to say, however, that Evangelina is not here today. It is a shame for she would very much love the scheme."

"That is quite alright," Mr. Garrett began. "I have asked Miss Hamilton to—"

"Georgia, dearest, would you not take Mr. Garrett for a walk around the grounds?" her mother said. "That way his trip here is not completely wasted."

"It is not a waste, ma'am," Mr. Garrett insisted. "Miss Hamilton has already agreed to join me."

"Yes, but poor Evangelina will be so disappointed if she could not go," Mrs. Hamilton pouted. "Georgia, are not the cherry trees in bloom?"

"No, mamma. It is too late into spring. The flowers fell off weeks ago."

Her mother cleared her throat. "Those trees are pretty nonetheless. You should show them to him." She flashed her eyes at Georgia who conceded.

"Yes, mamma," Georgia replied with a forced smile. "Give me a moment to grab a bonnet, Mr. Garrett." She quickly left her mother with him, half embarrassed by her mother's dismissal of her, and grabbed her favorite bonnet out of her room. She paused at a mirror on her way back out and sighed.

It would not have mattered if her bonnet was the most spectacular in the world; she would still never be as beautiful as her sister, and, therefore, at least in her mother's eyes, would never be as important. She sighed again at her plain reflection, taking a moment to at least fix her hair and straighten her posture before she plastered a smile on her face and went back downstairs.

Mr. Garrett and her mother were still waiting for her, her mother talking the poor young man's ear off to the point he almost looked relieved to see her descending the stairs. She stifled a laugh at the scene.

"Ah, there she is!" her mother exclaimed when she saw her. "Georgia often walks the grounds and knows all about the flowers and trees planted hereabouts. I am sure you will find pleasure in it."

Mr. Garrett gave a slight bow.

As Mr. Garrett walked out of the door, Mrs. Hamilton took her daughter aside a moment. "Do be on your best behavior, Georgia," she whispered. "Do not ruin your sister's chances of an illustrious marriage by talking unnecessarily. Not all men appreciate your crude sense of humor."

Georgia forced another smile. "Yes, mamma."

"You are a good girl," her mother told her. "Do show Mr. Garrett the orchard. It is quite lovely."

Georgia huffed as she walked out the door into the graying

sunshine where Mr. Garrett was waiting for her. He was very handsome. So handsome that Georgia kept forgetting just how handsome he was until she saw him again. It was as if his level of handsome was almost too impossible to be real and if he was not immediately before you, the memory of it would be like that of a fading dream.

It did not bother her, however. Though he was the chiseled image of a Greek god, her confidence did not waiver around him. He was not for her and, therefore, posed no threat. There was no chance of him ever seeing her as anything more than anyone else in the neighborhood did. Evangelina's opinionated elder sister, the unfortunate looking one.

She smiled comfortably at Mr. Garrett. "Shall we begin?"

He nodded, holding out his hand for her to lead the way.

"I am sorry your plans for a phaeton ride came to nothing," she told him. "It would have been a nice day for it."

"They did not have to come to nothing," he replied. "I would not have minded if it were you riding with me."

Georgia appreciated his kindness. "Yes, but I do know my sister would have been disappointed if she had not been able to go."

"You are very different from your mother and sister," Mr. Garrett told her. "I do not see much of a likeness between the three of you."

"Yes, I believe I take after some distant aunt," Georgia said with a sigh. "Her portrait is probably hidden away in the attic collecting dust and being eaten by rats."

He chuckled. "That is not what I meant," he explained. "You and your mother and sister are very different in character."

She glanced at him for a moment. "Yes, I have always thought so," she replied cautiously. "I tend to take after my father."

Mr. Garrett nodded. "It is the same with my sister," he told her. "She takes after our father more than I ever have. I believe I have more traits of my mother. She was a very kind, forgiving person." He smiled, remembering. "And the most understanding person I shall ever know."

"Are those the traits you believe you have inherited from her or just the ones you credit her the most for?" Georgia asked half teasing.

Mr. Garrett grinned at her. "I am not sure," he replied. "I just know I am more than the stoic man my father was."

There was a brief pause between them.

"Is your sister married, then?" she asked.

He nodded. "She lives in Bath with her husband and daughter."

There was another short lull in conversation.

"The other day at the ball, you mentioned your fondness for reading," she remembered.

"Yes."

"And what does a man like you, Mr. Garrett, read?"

He laughed through his nose. "A man like me?" he repeated. "I am not sure how I am to answer such a question. Are you asking *what does a man of my character read?* Or are you asking *what a man of my rank and birth reads?*"

"Oh, I am sure if we went with the latter, we would both be bored to tears!" Georgia proclaimed. "No, I will have no talk of genealogy or the history of how your money was made."

Mr. Garrett laughed.

"Let us go with a man of your character," she continued. "What does he read?"

"I enjoy histories," he began, "but I am not one to shy away from a novel."

She feigned a small gasp and made a face. "Novels?" she repeated in a tone much like her mother's. "Those will liquify your brain and turn you to nonsense! Novels are for silly girls and boys!"

Mr. Garrett smirked at her. "Is that an impression of your mother?"

"Spot on, I believe. And almost a direct quote."

He laughed. "I take it she does not approve?"

"She is not as fond of reading as I am."

He bobbed his head. "I recently read a book you might like. It is a gothic romance reminiscent of *The Mysteries of Udolpho.*"

"Oh?" Georgia replied cautiously.

He furrowed his brow for a moment. "What was it called? It is about a young girl who is orphaned and taken to her eccentric uncle's island where he has a castle and every night she swears she is visited by the ghost of a young woman."

Georgia smiled, pressing her lips together as Mr. Garrett described her own book to her.

"I am doing a poor job of describing the story to you, but it is captivating."

"Do you happen to remember who wrote it?"

"It was published under a pseudonym, Lady H."

"How mysterious," she said in a playful tone. "What could that stand for, I wonder?"

He cast her a questioning look. "I have brought the book with me if you would like to borrow it." He shook his head. "What is its name? I cannot believe I have forgotten."

"It is quite windy out," Georgia commented, pressing a hand to her bonnet. "Do you think the winds are coming from the west?" She looked around her as if searching for the answer.

Mr. Garrett shook his head. "The wind is not so terrible. Would you like to turn back?"

Georgia laughed. "No, never mind."

The next hour and a half passed by more pleasantly than Georgia could have expected. Half of her truly dreaded the walk she was going to take with Mr. Garrett knowing that it would inevitably lead to questions about her sister. However, to her surprise, Evangelina's name never came up.

When Mr. Garrett talked, he talked to her. And what he talked about was meant to interest them both. There was no talk about what her sister likes to do, or what her favorite color or flower was. That is what she was used to. Men always asked about her sister, but this was different.

It was just her and Mr. Garrett talking and laughing like old friends.

"The phaeton ride," Mr. Garrett began.

Georgia looked at him. "Yes?"

"I was honestly hoping you—"

"There you both are!" exclaimed her sister walking around the corner of the garden.

Both Mr. Garrett and Georgia jumped, half startled.

"Mamma told me you set out on a walk almost two hours ago," she continued playfully scolding. "She was beginning to worry."

Georgia smiled at her sister. "We did walk around, but ended up back here," she replied.

"Would you like to stay for dinner, Mr. Garrett?" her sister asked ignoring her. "Mamma has told me to ask."

"I would be delighted," he replied.

Evangelina flashed him her brightest smile. "Did Georgia show you our koi pond?" she asked him.

He glanced at Georgia. "No, I believe we became too involved with what we were talking about."

"Well, come, I shall show you," Evangelina told him. "It is perfectly situated."

Georgia stood from the bench. "I shall tell mamma you will be joining us for dinner," she said, knowing that she would no longer be wanted or needed.

"It was a pleasure, Miss Hamilton." Mr. Garrett gave her a bow and moved to follow her sister. "*The Winds of Westbrook!*" he half shouted, turning back around.

Georgia blushed at the name of her book while Evangelina seemed startled by the outburst.

"What?" Georgia called back.

"That is the name of the book I recently read." He then turned and continued his walk with Evangelina.

Georgia sighed as she watched them move along the brick path to another part of the garden. At least if he married her sister, she would have a companionable brother-in-law.

Dinner had gone well, very well, as far as Mrs. Hamilton was concerned. Mr. Garrett seemed to enjoy the food and did not shy away from an invitation to whist afterwards. Even Mr. Hamilton seemed invested in their guest.

As whist only allowed four players, Georgia opted to sit out. She left the party of four to their game and instead, found a place on the sofa with a book, which she found almost too difficult to read as the others barely stopped talking long enough to breathe.

Georgia constantly heard Mr. Garrett being encouraged to play as he seemed rather distracted and not paying attention to his hand. How could he, her mother would muse later, when Evangelina was placed directly across from him?

There were even a few times Georgia would look up to find him starring at her. Most likely to try and understand how two sisters, not far in age could look so different. Despite the wonderful hour and a half they spent together earlier that day, Georgia was rather glad to see him go. She felt a little too scrutinized over.

"Evangelina, we must visit him at his aunt and uncle's for tea soon," their mother said as they waved him goodbye. "He has obviously done you quite a service visiting you twice in such a small amount of time." Mrs. Hamilton gave a triumphant 'humph'. "How pleased I am things are progressing so quickly. He is sure to propose before he goes back to," she paused, "well, wherever he is from."

"Cornwall," Georgia added nonchalantly.

There was a pause.

"Cornwall, did you say?" Mrs. Hamilton repeated. "I thought I heard he was from Cambridge."

"He schooled there and even lived there for an extra year or two after, but, no, he is from Cornwall," Georgia clarified.

"Oh, dear," Mrs. Hamilton mumbled.

"Of all places, Cornwall?" Evangelina sighed. "Does he have an estate in Cornwall? Or is he merely leasing?"

Georgia felt a laugh rising out of her and coughed to suppress it.

She glanced at her father who seemed too deep in thought to join in on her fun.

"Does his being from Cornwall make him that much less attractive?" Georgia asked. "I believe he mentioned he has a house in town if that makes it better."

"Yes, but Cornwall?" Evangelina repeated.

"What is wrong with Cornwall?" Georgia pressed. "I have heard it is lovely."

Mr. Hamilton gave a small nod. "Well, I am for bed," he replied off topic as he turned into the house.

"Eight thousand a year is a wonderful income," Mrs. Hamilton said, reassuring herself.

Georgia took in a deep breath and let it out slowly before she followed her father's example and went inside.

5

A few days later, Georgia received another letter from William Henry. She could feel herself blush from her toes to her forehead when the servant handed it to her, her breath catching in her lungs as she gazed at the familiar handwriting.

"Who is that from?" Evangelina asked, noticing her sister's reaction.

"It is just from Louisa," Georgia quickly replied.

"If it is only from her, then why are you blushing?"

"Probably because it is stifling in this room," her mother replied for her, fanning herself.

"Yes," Georgia readily agreed. "It is quite stuffy. Shall I open a window, mamma?" She stood, eager to get away from her sister's prying eyes.

"Yes, please," her mother gratefully begged.

Georgia whisked to the window and threw it open. A light, pleasant breeze immediately filled the room.

"It is unusually hot for early May," Mrs. Hamilton complained taking in the fresh air as it glided through the room.

Georgia once again agreed, rocking back and forth on her feet for several seconds. "Well, I shall be in my room if anyone needs me," she added unnecessarily as she left, knowing full well neither of the women really cared.

Once she was safely within her room, she gently broke the seal to her letter and greedily took in its contents.

Miss Hamilton, Miss Georgia,

What joy I have received upon reading your response to my letter. I had been in utter turmoil the past few days since I had sent it, hoping you had not interpreted my lack of correspondence as a lack of feeling. I would, of course, hope by my now, that my feelings are understood. If they are not, then it is my duty to remind you.

I often sit and try to remember the sound of your laugh. It was such a wonderful sound and I wished with every fiber of my being that I was the one that had conjured it from your lips.

I sigh often when I think of it. Its remembrance touching my heart more than anything has ever done so before. The next we meet, all I want to do is make you laugh, so the joy that pours from you may also fill me. I was too shy to try my hand at it when first we met, but never again. I shall take encouragement from your letters.

Pray, tell me all that amuses you and they will be my constant study. For it is my life's mission to never see a frown upon your shining face. I will forever strive to do what it takes to make you, not only smile, but laugh.

Yours affectionately,

William Henry

Georgia sighed and wiped a tear she had not realized had formed from her eye. How was it possible that anyone could write such beautiful words? And how was it possible that those words were directed toward her? Even after almost a year's correspondence, she still found it a little surreal.

Not wanting the feeling of being noticed to end, she immediately pulled out her stationary and began her reply.

William,

You certainly flatter me too much as you always do. I consider myself a modest person, but your kind, beautiful words have opened a door to my vanity that I did not know existed and I am always eager to hear more.

I was not aware that I could ever have such a hold on someone until you came along, my kind, sweet William. Even after all of this time, however, I still find myself both perplexed and moved by you. Your eagerness to please has a mirrored effect and has left me with the same desire toward you. I wish to know more about you, your likes and dislikes, your dreams and aspirations.

As for myself, I am a voracious reader and am amused by all things ridiculous. There is nothing like a walk while the morning air is crisp, and the mist and fog are still hovering over the land like a secret whispered into the ear of a lover.

Georgia blushed at the last line. It was slightly out of character for her, and she did not know why she wrote it. Part of her wished to cross it out or start over, but after reading it once more, decided it was the most honest statement she had ever made, and kept it.

She continued her letter, describing her favorite books and plays and asking him in turn if he had any favorites. She poured into the letter a few of her hopes and wishes; things that she barely ever told herself.

She signed off after two pages of poetic response, eager to hear from him again.

Could she call him a lover? Could one make love, or fall in love via letter?

It is true, she had met him before, but, again, they barely said more than a few words to each other in person. Most of what she knew of him were from his letters and all of them combined might have equaled a few hours' conversation.

She shook her head. No, she knew what it meant to write. She knew that there was more feeling and passion in the written word- within these letters- than anything they could have said in person. Writing comes from the heart, and that was what was in their letters to one another. Heart.

Things were going to change for her. She might not be the beauty her sister was, but she was capable of capturing the heart and imagination of a man.

6

Ross Fairgrove came to visit the next day while Evangelina and Mrs. Hamilton were having tea at the Dorsets visiting Mr. Garrett. He was led into the parlor where Georgia was sitting at the writing desk and absent-mindedly staring out the window. Her journal was open, and her quill hovered over the pages.

She smiled at her friend when he entered. "I have not seen you since the ball," she said moving from the window seat to one of the sofas.

"Yes, I have been rather poor company as of late," he mumbled. "What are you writing? Another one of your stories? Is there a new novel to come out for Lady H?"

She sighed. "Hardly." She relaxed into her seat, her body seeming to melt into the cushions. "I cannot seem to focus on anything long enough to write. I feel as if all of my ideas have been dried up before I can even write them on paper."

"That is a shame. Your publisher will be asking for another man-uscript soon."

She sat up straight and smiled. "I must thank you again for all your help with facilitating everything between myself and Harvey and Browning's Publishing Company. I would never have been able to do this on my own." She stared down for a moment at her hands. "You do not know what it means to me."

"I do, which is why I agreed to help you." He dug into his pocket and retrieved a bank note. "This is for you, before I forget."

Georgia took the bank note and stared down at it with glisten-ing eyes. "Eight pounds! If my novel keeps this up, I could afford to keep myself!"

"You would never afford yourself with as many books as you buy, or paper you waste scratching out ideas."

She laughed. "Perhaps you are right, but it is a start."

Ross glanced around the room before focusing on the door.

"She is not here, Ross," Georgia told him. "She is having tea with the Dorests and Mr. Garrett."

He huffed. "And I am sure that is going well," he replied a little bitterly.

Georgia arched a brow at him. "I do feel for you, Ross," she began, "but I am sure one cannot help whom we do or do not have feelings for. You cannot blame Evangelina for the way she feels."

Ross shook his head. "I do not blame your sister."

Georgia frowned in confusion. "Do you blame yourself then?"

"No, I blame—" He stopped himself. "Forgive me. I did not come here to be moody. I came here for the pleasure of your company."

"You do not have to lie to *me*, Ross," Georgia muttered. "You came here for Evangelina." She sighed a little exasperatedly. "Just as every-one does."

Ross frowned. "Who is everyone?" he asked.

Georgia laughed gently at him. "I meant in general." She shook her head. "After your sister left, my visitations dwindled to practically none."

He nodded. "Would you like to take a walk?" he asked after a moment.

Georgia hesitated and tilted her head as she thought. "Are you going to wear that look of disappointment on your face the entire time, or are you going to at least pretend you will enjoy my company?"

Ross laughed. "I do not need to pretend to enjoy your company, Georgia," he told her. "I promise I actually do."

"Good," Georgia said with a smirk. "Then, you can escort me around the garden."

Ross did as he was told and led her outside with an actual smile. She told him of her much-awaited trip to his sister's in three months' time.

"I have not seen her since her wedding day and I feel as if I have been lost ever since," Georgia told him. "It is a shame to have your dearest friend so far away."

"Yes, how awful it is to no longer have a friend at your disposal," Ross teased.

Georgia nudged him. "That does not go without saying your company is most appreciated."

"I am just not my sister," he concluded for her.

Georgia lifted a brow at him. "Nor am I mine."

He sighed.

"What happened between the two of you?" she prodded gently. "A year ago, I would have sworn you would be married by now. The two of you were almost inseparable. Now, it is as if my sister is," she paused, "almost indifferent. Angry even sometimes when she sees you."

Ross straightened his back and cleared his throat.

"Was there a disagreement between the two of you?"

He took in a deep breath and let it out in a huff. "No, not between us," he replied a little begrudgingly. "Not one that should matter at any rate."

She looked at him curiously.

"I believe it was an influence that has separated your sister from me, not a disagreement."

"An influence?" she repeated.

Ross shook his head. "It is a subject I would not wish to get into for several reasons," he replied.

Georgia nodded. "I understand."

They moved to return, changing the subject of conversation. As they came to the front of the house, a man on a horse came racing up the drive, startling them. The man jumped off and straightened his jacket, a smug look on his face. Georgia recognized him at once as the man from the Dorset's ball.

"Can I help you, sir?" Georgia asked as the man seemed to almost stumble towards the front door.

He turned and Georgia could see he was very likely drunk. "Ah, you must be Evangelina's sister," he surmised.

"I am Miss Hamilton, yes," she replied a little tartly at his impertinence.

"I have come to visit Miss Evangelina."

Ross tensed. "She is not home, Talbot."

"And how should you know, Fairgrove?" he challenged unnecessarily. "Are you her keeper?"

Ross's face reddened with anger.

"He is not," Georgia replied gently, but forcefully. "But he is right. My sister is at tea with our mother. They are visiting the Dorsets."

Mr. Talbot sucked his teeth. "Is that so?"

"Yes," Georgia confirmed. "They left a little over an hour ago and are not expected back until just before supper."

Mr. Talbot nodded thoughtfully. "Very well then," he replied with an awkward bow. "Do mind telling Evangelina that I called." He turned just as elegantly and mounted his horse before leaving in a cloud of dust.

Georgia blushed at the use of her sister's Christian name by this stranger and exchanged a concerned glance with Ross.

"That man is a disease," he grumbled.

She nodded. "He can certainly bring nothing but trouble," she agreed. "To call on my sister in such a state! I am offended for her!"

"Will you tell her?"

Georgia thought for a moment. "I do not see why I should not," she replied. "I should most certainly want to know if a potential suitor of mine called on me while inebriated. It is not very genteel of him."

Ross nodded. "I think I should go," he told her after a moment. "My mother will be waiting for me."

Georgia smiled somberly. "I shall call on you soon. Thank you for walking with me."

Ross bowed. "It is always a pleasure, Georgia. I do mean that. You have always been a good friend."

Georgia pressed another smile on her face.

Until her letters from William Henry, that is all she has ever been to anybody. A friend.

GEORGIA RELATED THE MISHAP WITH MR. TALBOT TO HER SISTER later that evening, catching her alone in front of her vanity not soon after she returned home. Georgia entered her sister's room and shut the door behind her, causing her sister to turn and give her a strange look. Though they were not far in age, they had never truly been close which made this tete-a-tete rather out of character.

"What are you doing?" Evangelina asked her.

"I have something of a delicate nature to talk to you about," Georgia replied, "and I did not want mamma or any of the servants to overhear."

Evangelina perked up. "Are you sharing gossip with me?"

Georgia shook her head. "Not really. I am hopefully ending what could turn into rather unpleasant gossip."

Evangelina pouted. "Well, that is no fun." She turned back to her vanity.

"Gossip about you, Lina."

Evangelina met her sister's gaze in the mirror but didn't turn around to face her.

"Mr. Talbot stopped by the house this afternoon hoping to call on you."

Georgia noticed the color in her sister's cheeks rise and a strange sparkle appeared in her eyes.

"I am not clear on what your feelings are for this man, but I must advise you that an attachment to him would be very unwise."

Evangelina narrowed her eyes at her sister. "And what would you know about it?" she almost growled.

Georgia took a deep breath. "While he was not completely obscene, he was rather drunk, Lina, as well as abrasive toward Ross."

"Ross?" she repeated in a heightened voice. "What does he have to do with any of it?"

"Ross came for a visit and witnessed the whole scene," Georgia replied. "Mr. Talbot, who seems to want for a closer relationship with you, is not a man I would wish for you."

Evangelina scoffed and shook her head. "Am I to receive suitor advice from someone who will most likely never have one herself?"

Georgia's breath caught in her throat and her stomach dropped painfully, but she refused to show her sister any reaction to her harsh words. "I am not giving you advice as someone who has known love," she retorted, "but as a sister who only wishes the best for you."

Evangelina paused in fixing her hair to lock eyes with her sister in the mirror again. "Like, Mr. Garrett?" she asked.

Georgia blinked at her a moment before shaking her head. "No, if he is not who you want, I would not wish you to be with him, though he seems a perfect gentleman."

Evangelina shifted her gaze. "Did Mr. Talbot say anything when he came?"

Georgia opened her mouth to speak but paused a moment, a little confused. "I am not sure what difference that should make."

"It makes all the difference, Georgia," Evangelina whispered in an angry tone.

Georgia shook her head. "No," she finally replied. "He did not say anything substantial. He just wanted me to let you know he called."

Evangelina nodded.

"Nothing good could come of an acquaintance with him, Lina," she told her sister softly.

"What did Ross say?" Evangelina said, ignoring her.

Georgia blinked, slightly confused. "Nothing," she replied. "I did all of the talking."

Evangelina let out an audible sigh. "Thank you for you the warning, Georgia," she said with little feeling. "But, I stand firm in my conviction that you know nothing of what you speak. Please leave my room."

"Lina, do not think I am ignorant to the wiles of men just because—"

Evangelina laughed. "The wiles of men," she repeated. "How ridiculous you sound, Georgie. Where do you get such notions? From those silly books you spend your days reading? Or perhaps the ones you spend hours trying to write?"

Georgia tried not to scowl at her sister. "My advice was meant kindly," she stated firmly. "If you are to ignore it all because I have never been openly courted, then you are a fool and it shows more than just a lack of intelligence on your part, but an immature arrogance that is uglier than anything I have seen!"

"Even your own face?" Evangelina asked with a sneer.

Georgia felt herself pale. "Yes, Lina," she retorted, standing taller. "Even my face." She turned without another word and walked out the door, her chest tight with anger and pain.

7

GEORGIA, HAVING ANXIOUSLY WAITED FOR A REPLY FROM WILLIAM FOR what seemed like an eternity, was disappointed once again by a lack of response in the mail. She sighed to herself when nothing more than a letter for her father was delivered.

Dutifully, however, she walked the letter to her father's study where he was looking rather forlorn and tired. Upon seeing her, he perked up, a warm smile spreading over his face.

"Good afternoon, my dear," he said in greeting.

"Good afternoon, papa," Georgia replied. "Here is a letter for you." She proffered it to him which he took almost hesitantly. She watched as his expression changed. "Is something wrong?"

Her father shook his head. "I am fine," he reassured her with a less than convincing smile. "Do run along and pour me a glass of port, would you?"

"Papa," she hesitated, chuckling lightly, "it is quite early, do you not think?"

He gave his daughter a somewhat stern look. "Georgie, do not get in the habit of telling everyone their business," he warned. "It is not a desirable trait in anyone."

She bowed her head. "Yes, papa. I shall grab you some port right away then."

"Good girl." He waited for her to leave the room before he opened his letter and sighed in desperate exasperation.

Georgia walked into the parlor after delivering her father's port looking for her book. Her sister was busy retrimming a bonnet, while her mother played cards by herself at a small table. Her sister, who had not spoken to her since their conversation about Mr. Talbot the day before, acknowledged her presence by barely looking up from what she was doing; Mrs. Hamilton at least grumbled a 'hello, dear'.

Once she located her book, Georgia found a vacant sofa and sat down. She sat on the couch perfectly poised- just as anyone would expect a lady of her class to do- and flipped through the pages until she found where she had left off. She smiled to herself as she read, content with the world she had entered.

Evangelina laughingly scoffed. "What could you possibly be smiling about?"

Georgia looked up at her sister. "I did not realize I was smiling," she replied. "Does it bother you so much?"

"Girls," their mother said in a warning tone still concentrating on her solitary game of cards, "must you start something every day?"

Evangelina huffed while Georgia resumed her book.

Not long after, a young servant girl walked into the room with a huge grin on her face. She hurriedly walked over to their mother and whispered in her ear. Mrs. Hamilton's eyes grew wide with joy as she stood from her table.

"Oh, Lina, he is here again!" she exclaimed.

"Who, mamma?" Evangelina asked.

"Mr. Garrett!" she exclaimed rushing over to her youngest daughter and pinching her cheeks to bring more color to them. "Look alive, child!"

Georgia shook her head at the ridiculous display before her as she flipped the next page of her book.

Evangelina gently pushed her mother's hands from her face. "I am sure I do not need any help securing him, mamma," she reassured her a little too arrogantly. "He has already been here to see me twice this week. It should be no time at all before he makes me an offer."

Georgia huffed and soon after, Mr. Garrett was introduced into the room. The women stood and curtseyed.

He bowed elegantly. "Good afternoon, Mrs. Hamilton, Miss Hamilton, and Miss Evangelina," he said. "I hope I am not intruding on anything of importance."

"Oh, no intrusion at all," Mrs. Hamilton told him. "You are quite welcome, Mr. Garrett."

Georgia smiled as Mr. Garrett's eyes fell on her.

"It is a beautiful day for a ride, and I was wondering if I could entice Miss—"

"Oh, a ride does sound lovely," Evangelina told him. "I have been sitting for too long. Allow me a minute to change and I will join you."

Mr. Garrett blinked, his mouth slightly open for a moment, glancing between the two sisters. "Would you not like to join us, Miss Hamilton?" he asked slowly.

Georgia readjusted her glasses. "Well, actually I—"

"Georgia is not one for riding," Evangelina finished for her. "She prefers books to people and the outdoors."

Georgia narrowed her eyes slightly at her sister. "That is hardly true. I am always out walking the grounds. But she is right on one thing. I am not a great rider."

"Perhaps we could walk then," Mr. Garrett suggested.

"Oh, I am sure Georgia has something better to do. Do you not, dear?" Mrs. Hamilton asked.

Georgia frowned at her mother. "Actually, I do not have anything better to do," she replied defiantly, putting the book she was still holding on an end table. "A walk would do me good. I have yet to go outside today."

Mr. Garrett grinned.

"Are you sure you would not rather ride, Mr. Garrett?" Evangelina urged. "It is what you first came over to do."

"No, I would not wish to exclude your sister," he replied firmly.

Georgia smiled in appreciation.

The weather was indeed fine. The sun was warm, but the subtle breeze made the air pleasant. This was commented on for several minutes by the threesome as they walked along one of the lanes.

Georgia could feel the awkwardness and felt that it was her intrusion that was causing it, but she refused to care. She had just as much right to take a walk as anyone did.

"Are you here for much longer, Mr. Garrett?" Evangelina asked.

"I believe I am here for the summer," he replied.

"Do you like it here then?"

He nodded. "Yes, it is a very pleasant town."

Georgia tried not to yawn.

"Have you made it to town yet?" Evangelina pressed. "With all of the shops?"

"I have been by them, but never stopped in."

"Oh, I often meet friends in the tea rooms," she explained. "Georgia often loses herself in the bookshop."

Georgia refrained from rolling her eyes.

"Is there one in town?" Mr. Garrett asked, his interest finally sounding piqued.

Evangelina nodded. "Yes, it is right across the street from the Lion's Mane Inn. It's a dingy, dusty little place."

"I shall have to see for myself," he replied. "Are the books of good quality there?" he asked Georgia ripping her from her reverie.

"I beg your pardon?" she asked, half dazed.

Evangelina sighed. "He wants to know if the book shop has any good books."

"Oh, yes," she replied. "Most of them come from traveling libraries but you are able to order anything you like. I recently ordered a book my cousin recommended. *Frankenstein.*"

Mr. Garrett looked surprised. "I have read it," he replied. "It is chilling."

"No more so than *The Monk*, I am sure," Georgia gushed.

"Have you read that?" he replied. "It is one of my favorites."

Evangelina regarded the both of them in utter confusion as they continued to discuss books of which she had never nor would ever read. It bored her almost to distraction and after several minutes of listening to the two of them drag on, she yawned loudly lest she be forgotten completely.

"Forgive us," Mr. Garrett apologized half-heartedly. "We seem to have excluded you from the conversation."

"It is no bother," Evangelina claimed. "I was wondering, however, if you would mind stopping in on the Hayes sisters."

Georgia caught herself before she groaned.

"You would like to visit Miss Jennifer and Miss Jessica Hayes?" Mr. Garrett replied.

"Oh, yes, it would a great surprise to them," Evangelina urged.

Mr. Garrett looked unsure, casting a glance at Georgia in the hopes of a reply.

"Evangelina," her sister said gently, "perhaps, we could instead save that trip for another day. We should be turning back soon."

"Nonsense! If we go now, then we shall be invited to dinner," Evangelina pointed out.

"Three extra plates for dinner on short notice might not be so welcome," Georgia commented. "It might seem more like an intrusion."

Evangelina hesitated. "Then we will just stay for a few minutes," she compromised.

Georgia opened her mouth to protest but, deciding she did not care either way, conceded.

"Come, Mr. Garrett," Evangelina said, looping her arm in his and directing him away from her sister. "The twins would love to get better acquainted with you."

Georgia followed behind the other two unsure as to why she felt she needed to participate in the impending display of pretentious superciliousness, but as she had decided when they first began their walk, she was determined.

On first arriving at the Hayes's once-luxurious manor that was now slowly falling into disrepair, they were met with wonderous surprise. The smirks that decked the faces of the twins as they walked in were almost unbearable to Georgia, especially when paired with their identical shrill giggling.

Georgia did not like the twins. Even before she caught them talking about her at the Dorsets's ball, she found them rather odd and had never seemed to be comfortable in their presence. Their piercing blue eyes always seemed to burrow under her skin and make it crawl, as if they were cats on the prowl for a mouse.

"We are very honored that you have come out of your way to visit us, Mr. Garret," Jennifer Hayes said, a slight blush coloring her cheeks.

"Yes, we thought we were going to pass the rest of the afternoon in utter boredom," Jessica added, not wanting to be out done by her sister.

Mr. Garrett bowed. "The pleasure is all mine," he told them dutifully, though Georgia got the feeling the visit was no pleasure at all.

"We would have been over sooner," Evangelina informed them, "but as Mr. Garrett was so kind as to invite my sister along, we decided to walk rather than ride."

Everyone's eyes in the room turned to Georgia, most of them accusingly. She smiled in return showing how little she cared for their disdain.

"That was very kind of you to invite poor Georgia," Jessica said.

"Yes, very kind," Jennifer agreed.

"I'm sorry, did you say 'poor Georgia'?" Mr. Garrett asked, confused. Georgia frowned.

"Did I say that?" Jessica asked her twin.

"No, I do not believe so," Jennifer replied. "You must have heard her incorrectly, Mr. Garret. Do speak up when you talk, Jessica."

"Yes, I do tend to speak too softly sometimes," Jessica replied.

There was an awkward pause after this.

"Shall you stay for dinner?" the twins said in unison, causing Georgia to shudder.

"How gracious of an invitation," Evangelina started.

"However," Georgia cut in, "we must unfortunately decline."

The twins slowly turned their gaze on her.

"We are expected home and only stopped in for a quick visit," Georgia finished. She was not sure, but she thought she noticed the twins narrow their eyes at her, albeit, only for a moment.

"What a shame," Jessica claimed. "Is it not, Jennifer?"

"Yes, a pity," Jennifer agreed. "For we were expecting another guest and it would have been great fun to have you all."

The two of them exchanged mischievous glances.

"Mr. Talbot should be here any moment," Jessica said in triumph.

Evangelina paled for a moment before turning red. Georgia felt her stomach drop at the mention of the name.

"Georgia, I do not see why we cannot stay and enjoy a nice evening with the Hayes and their guest," Evangelina said. "Mamma did not necessarily say we must return home for supper."

"If you stay, we shall order the carriage to take you home," Jennifer suggested.

"Then you should not have to walk in the dark," Jessica concluded.

Mr. Garrett, who was unable to find a suitable moment to say anything before, finally spoke up. "Unfortunately, I cannot stay. My aunt has invited dinner guests of our own and I am afraid I must attend."

The twins pouted.

"In fact, I believe I must return soon to retrieve my horse from the Hamilton's to be home on time."

Evangelina looked a little put out.

"Do not fret on my account," he told her. "Please, stay and enjoy your friends." He turned to Georgia. "I shall, if you would prefer, escort you home, Miss Hamilton."

Georgia looked at her sister and then the twins whose posture told her she was nothing more than an unwanted soul drifting in their house. She smiled at Mr. Garrett. "Thank you, sir, I think I shall accept your company." She glanced at her sister again who was actively avoiding her eye. "Are you sure you will not return with us, Lina?" she pressed.

Evangelina still did not look at her. "No, thank you, Georgia, I shall stay and return later in the Hayes's carriage."

Georgia was ashamed for her sister's behavior, abandoning Mr. Garrett when he had come to visit with her. She looked to see how he bore it, but his face was indiscernible.

"Then we shall take leave of you," Georgia said as she rose. She and Mr. Garrett thanked the twins and left the house in considerable silence, walking almost a quarter of a mile before saying anything.

"The Hayes sisters seem pleasant," Mr. Garrett ventured slowly.

Georgia arched a brow at him. "I am worried your definition of pleasant is far from mine, Mr. Garrett," she replied.

He laughed. "They are not friends of yours?"

Georgia did not like talking poorly about others, but she could not deny her dislike of the twins. "They are not *my* particular friends, no," she replied. "But they do follow my sister around relentlessly."

"Who are your friends then?" he asked. "Mr. Fairgrove?"

"Ross?" she said. "Yes, he is a good friend. I have known his family since infancy. His sister and I are particularly close."

"I was unaware he had a sister."

"She married last year and moved around thirty miles north of here," she told him.

He nodded.

"I am to visit her soon."

"Thirty miles north? That would be Derbyshire?"

"That is right."

"I have a friend who married last year from there," Mr. Garrett said. "Franklin Barker."

Georgia gaped at him a moment. "Why, that is Louisa's husband!" she exclaimed. "How incredible you should know him!"

"We went to Cambridge together. He is a very fine gentleman," Mr. Garrett said.

She nodded. "I heartily agree."

The rest of the walk was full of conversation about plays, music, sciences, and, surprisingly to Mr. Garrett, politics. He marveled in her conviction and understanding of subjects that even he tried to ignore.

"Where does your confidence come from, Miss Hamilton?" Mr.

Garrett asked her as they walked up the drive to her house.

Georgia looked at him surprised. "My confidence?" she repeated. She shook her head. "I was not aware that I had any."

He regarded her for a moment. "You exude it."

Georgia laughed at this strange portrayal of herself.

"I am being perfectly serious," he pressed. "I envy you it."

"*You* envy *me*?" she questioned almost skeptically.

He nodded. "If I had your confidence, I am sure there is not much I could not do."

Georgia smiled and looked down. "If I were a vainer person, Mr. Garrett, I would urge you to go on, but, as I am not used to compliments, I am at a loss for words."

"It is just—you impress me. The way you stand up for yourself," he continued. "I noticed it earlier today with your sister."

"Did you?" Georgia chuckled. "I am afraid you are mistaken. That is not confidence," she corrected. "That is just an aversion to superciliousness and arrogance, and my inability to keep my opinions to myself."

"Which takes a certain amount of confidence in yourself and your convictions, does it not?"

She smiled and nodded after thinking it over. "I suppose you are right. Thank you. I have never thought of it that way."

They stopped at the front of the house, looking at each other.

"I must apologize for my sister," she said, shifting her gaze.

He furrowed his brow and tilted his head slightly. "What for?"

"Well, that she stayed at the Hayes's when you came here to visit with her," she clarified. "I am not sure what would possess her to do something like that. She is not usually this thoughtless." Georgia was not sure why she kept lying to him about her sister.

"May I ask you a question?"

Georgia pursed her lips and nodded. "Yes."

"Why does everyone assume I come here to visit with your sister?"

Georgia was unable to answer the question as Mrs. Hamilton

appeared from around the corner of the house, clinging to her husband's arm.

"You are home!" her mother exclaimed, waving. "How was your walk?"

"Quite nice, Ma'am. Very beautiful country you have around here," Mr. Garrett commented.

"Thank you, sir," Mrs. Hamilton replied. "We are very proud of it, are we not, dear?"

Mr. Hamilton nodded. "I would say you would not find any finer, but I believe my opinion is more than a little bias."

Mrs. Hamilton, after noticing her youngest daughter was not with them, seemed a little confused. "Where is Evangelina? Is she already in the house?"

"Oh, no, mamma," Georgia replied slowly. "We stopped in on the twins and Evangelina decided to stay and dine with them."

A moment of appalment flashed across Mrs. Hamilton's face. "Did she?" she replied, rather composed. "And you did not urge her to return with you?"

"I tried but—"

"That is no matter," her mother cut her off. "Mr. Hamilton, would you not escort me inside? My feet are rather tired."

"Certainly."

"It is always a pleasure, Mr. Garrett," Mrs. Hamilton said as she passed. "Do come visit us again."

Mr. Garrett bowed.

Georgia suppressed a laugh at her mother's strange behavior. "Thank you for your company," she said to Mr. Garrett.

"It was indeed my pleasure," he replied. "I do so enjoy our conversations."

Georgia curtseyed to his bow.

"Good day, Mr. Garrett."

"Good day, Miss Hamilton."

Georgia smiled and made her way into the house where she was almost immediately accosted by her mother.

"How could you let her stay at the Hayes's?" she pressed. "What would possess her to do such a thing when she had Mr. Garrett by her side?"

Georgia sighed. "I am not entirely sure, mamma," she replied. "But she could not be persuaded to return home with us."

"Awful twins. This is part of their scheming," her mother surmised. "I just know it. Horrid creatures always sticking their noses in other people's business as if anyone cared two straws for them."

Georgia moved toward the stairs when she stopped. She thought for a moment that she should bring up Mr. Talbot and the possible attachment growing between him and her sister. She thought she should warn her mother of the imprudence of such a match. That the man was possibly a drunkard and good for nothing. She thought it would be best to divulge a potentially dangerous situation for her sister, but Georgia had stopped caring.

"Yes, mamma," she agreed instead. "The twins are rather awful."

8

Happily, and quickly did the word spread from the mouths of the Hayes sisters of the growing attachment between Mr. Garrett and their friend Evangelina Hamilton. Just as quickly did the word spread about how his kindness had no bounds and he would often include poor, plain Georgia on their walks, sacrificing what alone time he could be having with Evangelina to make sure her unfortunate sister did not feel left out.

Quickly and easily did the good opinion of Mr. Garrett rise, and more and more did the small-minded people of the small town of Barchester grow to favor the match between him and their pretty Evangelina Hamilton. Only someone good, and kind, and handsome—but also rich—could deserve the beautiful Evangelina, and everyone was satisfied that Mr. Garrett was that man.

The breakfast table was quiet, especially compared to the scene from the night before when Evangelina finally returned home from the Hayes's. Evangelina had come home a little later than would have deemed proper without an escort, a fact that her mother very quickly, though not as sternly as she should have, told her.

Evangelina, who Georgia observed was very likely drunk, gave her apologies, but the smile did not leave her face. Instead, she skipped her way up to her room, humming to herself. Georgia exchanged glances with her mother who appeared rather unnerved by the scene. It was, as usual and per society's rules, not discussed, but rather swept quickly and fervently under the rug. Nothing was an issue if you properly ignored it.

Evangelina yawned while she pushed around her food, a slight smile still strewn across her face leftover from the night before. It was an expression that was not lost on anyone and as soon as the servants left the room her father spoke.

"I have never seen you smile so early in the morning, Evangelina," he commented. "Is it due to what I assume was a pleasant evening last night?"

Evangelina blushed subtly. "Yes, papa," she replied dutifully. "I had a very wonderful time at the Hayes's. They are always very accommodating."

Mrs. Hamilton huffed. "I do not know how they can afford to be," she said bitterly. "Their father does nothing but throw his money away every chance he gets. Pretty soon, their manor Penwether will be nothing but rubble."

No one commented further, but Georgia noticed her father baulk at this.

"He is a very irresponsible man," Mrs. Hamilton added, deciding she was not done abusing the Hayes family.

Mr. Hamilton cleared his throat and wiped his mouth with a napkin.

"He is always sending his wife away on lavish holidays, but not a penny is spent on the repairs of that poor estate." She sighed. "It was once beautiful, you know?" She glanced up from her food for a moment to acknowledge her husband. "Oh, my dear, that does remind me, I wish to extend our time in London this season by a fortnight. I hope to be ahead of the fashion this year."

Mr. Hamilton sat frozen for a moment. "I am afraid we will not be able to go to town this season, dear," he sighed, finally realizing the façade he had been holding up was starting to crumble.

"What do you mean, George?" Mrs. Hamilton replied.

Their daughters looked up from their breakfasts, the silence of the moment only broken by the sounds of the cutlery scraping against the plates.

Mr. Hamilton cleared his throat. "There are going to be a few things we must economize on from here on out."

"What are you talking about, papa?" Evangelina asked. "What is the matter? Why should we be economizing?"

"Papa?" Georgia said softly when her father didn't answer.

Mr. Hamilton rubbed his mouth with his hand. "I have just had a letter from our bank yesterday," he stopped to swallow, "and it seems as if—that perhaps pretty soon—"

"Come out with it, George," his wife said impatiently.

"We are soon to be bankrupt," he finally told them.

The women gasped, forks clattering against their plates as all of them erupted into questions.

"What does that mean, papa? Are we now poor?" Evangelina wailed.

"Where did all our money go?" his wife shouted. "Are we to now beg for our food and lodgings?"

"What can be done, papa?" Georgia asked almost inaudibly next to her sister's and mother's cries. "How might we rectify this issue?"

Her father smiled at her and reached out to pat her hand. "It might take time, but I will find a way to make this right," he said. "Until then, we all must do what we can to help. No more shopping—"

Evangelina gasped. "Am I to wear all of my old dresses? Are we reduced to the rags of last year's fashions?"

"Evangelina, please, try to calm yourself," Georgia urged gently.

"That is easy for you to say!" Evangelina whined. "You're not pretty enough to care about what you wear."

Georgia averted her eyes, momentarily abashed by her sister's harsh words. "Perhaps not," she replied softly, "but I am at least mature enough to know when to put my own selfish needs aside for something more important, and smart enough to know when that time is. But I guess being a silly little girl has its advantages. Ignorance is bliss they say."

Evangelina scoffed.

"That is enough, girls!" their mother scolded. "We have enough problems without you squabbling."

"I understand this situation will take some time getting used to," Mr. Hamilton told them, his voice that of a defeated man, "but I know we can pull through. And, I am sorry for it, Evangelina, but anything that you have in your closet is good enough for you to wear, whether they be last year's fashion or not. New clothes are an expense we can do without."

Evangelina huffed, standing abruptly from the table before pushing her way out of the door. Mrs. Hamilton held her cross gaze on her husband for several moments without saying a word until she finally stood as well.

"You better make this right, George," she said in a low voice. "I will not see my children ruined." She then followed her youngest daughter out of the room, though with a lot less flourish.

Georgia reached out and squeezed her father's hand, seeing how the weight of the issue was wearing on him and had been for several days. "What has happened, papa?" she asked gently, without judgement in her voice.

George Hamilton buried his face in his other hand. "I have sunk almost all of our fortune into some rather risky investments," he replied. "I thought more about the reward and what it could offer you and Evangelina and your mother without any consideration to what we could lose."

"You have been speculating?"

Her father nodded.

Georgia searched the ever-deepening lines on her father's face, hoping for an answer. "Could you not take a mortgage out on the house, or—"

"No," he cut her off, shaking his head deeply. "I already have, and I am behind on those payments."

The blood drained from Georgia's face when the reality of the situation fully sunk in. "Then, we have nothing left?"

"There are still a few thousand pounds set aside for you and your sister as dowries. I thankfully did not take all of it."

She shook her head. "Papa, we will see this through. I can live in what clothes I already own. I can trade my books for new ones instead of buying-- or sell them if need be. We could sell some of our art and a few of the horses, perhaps even a carriage. We will find a way to right ourselves."

Mr. Hamilton smiled somberly at his daughter. "I do not deserve you, my dear," he told her.

Georgia regarded her father for a moment. "Is this why you were excited about Mr. Garrett when I told you about him? You saw him as a way out?"

Her father looked abashed. "You are too clever for me, Georgia." He nodded almost imperceptibly. "Yes, the thought of us being saved by him has crossed my mind," he confessed. "I am almost ashamed to say it out loud."

"There is no shame in wanting to save your family, papa," Georgia comforted him. "I am sure people have done worse for such a thing."

"Yes, I am sure they have, but it does not make my situation any less despicable. Using my daughter to fortune hunt for me?" He shook his head. "It is not sound."

"Do not fret, papa," she began. "Evangelina is capable of capturing the hearts of rich men. I believe Mr. Garrett is rather taken in with her. Otherwise, I cannot imagine why he would visit so much."

Her father nodded absent-mindedly. "Thank you, my child," he said as he rose from the table. "Now, if you do not mind, I will be in my office, wallowing in self-pity." He smiled suggesting he was trying to make light of the situation, but Georgia could see the torment reflecting in his eyes.

She sighed as she watched him leave. She sat for several minutes by herself, staring at the half eaten plate of food in front of her. She could hardly eat, but the thought of how different meals might look from now on made her shovel another spoonful into her mouth. She grimaced as she chewed, her mouth suddenly dry. She took a gulp of her tea to wash the food down before falling back into her chair.

A servant came in a minute later with a letter for her. Her heart fluttered at the sight of the handwriting, recognizing the hurried scribble of William Henry. She, as stoically as she could, received the letter and promptly put it in her pocket. She then rose calmly from the table and walked briskly to retrieve her bonnet before slipping outside.

She walked at a normal pace for several yards until she was sure no one was around. She then half ran, half skipped to her favorite spot under the large oak. She pulled out the letter, her cheeks rising in color as she broke the seal. Her breath catching in her throat as she read.

Dearest, loveliest Georgia,

I did not think you could grow more perfect until I read your last letter. A voracious reader, a lover of long walks, your poetic descriptions of the countryside. All these things are interests we share and next we meet, I hope to lose ourselves in conversation over books as we explore the fine roads of Barchester.

It surprises me, that a young woman such as you would not be used to beautiful words inspired by you when all you do is inspire them within me. You are indeed my muse and if I were a more talented man, I would spend my life trying to capture the warmth and beauty that has enveloped me since we first met in a painting so that your image would never be far from me.

I am sincerely counting down the days until we can meet again, and I am able to bask in the warmth of your many virtues. Until then, I will wait every day wishing for a letter full of well wishes from you.

Sincerely entranced,

William Henry

Georgia dabbed at a tear that was beginning to fall and kissed his signature. What was this swelling in her chest she got every time she read one of his beautiful letters? Why could she not wait until she received her next one? What inspired her to wish to further communicate with a man she barely knew? Was it love?

At that moment, she felt she deserved to be happy, and, however silly some might have found it, she felt at that moment she was. His letter was a welcome relief from the bitter news of her family's misfortunes, a brief reprieve from what must soon befall them. It gave her hope that she would not be a burden on her family because, soon, she too might be married. A wife! Just imagine!

After spending an hour or so sighing over her letter, Georgia thought it was proper to return to the house to write her reply. She wrote fervently, yet, cautiously, writing as any one lover would write to another with mixed emotions of elation and turmoil, overthinking every word. Was she writing too much? Was she not writing enough? Would he return a letter with an emotion equal to the one she was trying to convey?

This was how Georgia spent the chief of the morning, wondering with fevered anxiety as to how soon her letter would be received and how long after she would get a reply. It was not until a servant came to tell her that her mother was looking for her, did she realize how long she had locked herself away in her room reanalyzing her third- or, perhaps fourth- draft of a response.

Giving herself just one more minute, she quickly read through what she wrote and, being as satisfied as she could be, decided that what she had would do. It was not perfect, but it was how she felt.

Your letter can only be described as a single candle in the dead of the night, sending out its light and warmth into my world, said one phrase.

With each passing day, I grow to memorize your letters as they are as dear to me as any of my books. I read them constantly. They are my first thought in the morning and my last before I go to bed, read another.

She picked up her quill and gently dipped it, hesitating slightly as she wrote out her last line.

May the lips that caressed this page find yours.

Her cheeks flushed, as she wrote it and again as she read it over and over. She then pressed her lips to the paper and kissed it before signing her name and preparing it to be sent to William.

Georgia sighed and pressed her hand to her cheek as she thought of him reading and perhaps even kissing the spot where she had kissed. Her heart fluttered rapidly in her chest as she floated out of her bedroom door and right into a servant.

"Beg ya pardon, miss, but ma'am does ask ya to come down," the young woman said with a curtsey.

"Oh, Betty, I apologize," Georgia told her. "You did tell me. I am on my way. I was just trying to finish a letter. A letter to Louisa, my friend," she added unnecessarily.

"Very good, miss," Betty replied. "Shall I post it for ya?"

"Yes, would you be so kind?" Georgia asked, handing her the precious piece of paper.

Betty curtsied and dutifully took it. "Yes, miss."

Georgia nodded and made her way down to where Betty had told her the first time her mother was. She started as she entered the small parlor that faced the front of the house, her sister sitting pristinely on the edge of one of the sofas, her mother sitting on a chair a little more rigidly, while her father stood behind them staring blankly out the window. All of them with a different look of trepidation on their faces.

"I am so glad you could grace us with your presence, Georgia," her mother said sternly. "I hope we did not drag you from anything of importance."

"No, mamma," Georgia replied. "Betty did inform me you wished to see me. I apologize for any delay."

Her mother nodded. "Have a seat."

Georgia did as she was told.

"You are well aware what dire circumstances we are in," she began. "Our fortune now greatly diminished from what it was, there will be some great changes made to help us economize."

Georgia looked up at her father who could not meet her eyes.

"Your father and I have decided to use your dowry, Georgia, to pay off some of the debt owed."

Georgia's breath caught in her throat and her stomach dropped. "But, papa, I thought you said—"

"We also think it is time you start thinking about your future," her mother interrupted her.

Georgia searched the faces of the other people in the room, but no one, not even her sister would look at her. "What about my future?" she asked finally.

"We think it best, for the time being, that you employ yourself as a governess," her mother told her almost without feeling.

Georgia was stunned. She knew she had before thought of resigning herself to such a life, but to hear her mother so openly suggest it was almost unfathomable. To force your daughter into the employ of some other family, some other richer, more well-to-do family, was a sign that things were more dire than expected.

Georgia swallowed, her throat now dry with confusion and an overwhelming feeling of hopelessness. How could she just moments before have been elevated to the highest feelings of hope and happiness only to be plummeted into the dark pits of utter despair?

"I do not understand, mamma," she finally replied. "Does this decision have to be made now? Might it not be something we discuss further down the road?"

"Simply put, Georgia," her mother began, "we will soon not be able to care for you. It is the best for not only you, but for us as well. If you are taken care of, then that is less money we have to spend on your upkeep."

Georgia was stunned for a few seconds, but recollecting herself she shook her head. "I have money!" she almost shouted. "I have money of my own coming in!"

At this, everyone looked at her with curious surprise.

Georgia swallowed though her dry throat made it fruitless. "I have—I am—I wrote a book!" she finally said, her palms becoming sweaty with nervousness. "I had it published by a publisher in Oxford. Harvey and Browning."

Her family looked at her, dumbfounded.

"Ross went to school with the owner's nephew, and he was able to pass my novel off to them." She cleared her throat, her nervousness growing as her family continued to gape at her. "Mr. Harvey loved it and took it on."

"Ross helped you get your book published?" Evangelina asked.

"Georgia," her father whispered. "That is wonderful!"

Mrs. Hamilton exchanged glances with her husband. "You did this without our permission?" her mother asked, turning her attention back to her. "A woman in your station taking money—earning money! It is unheard of! Had I known you were accepting money for this, I would not have allowed it!"

Georgia gaped at her mother. "What does that signify now?" she asked. "You are sending me away to earn my keep now that we are ruined, so what would me earning a few pounds here and there matter had we maintained our fortune?"

Her mother stared at her coldly. "How much did this book you wrote make?"

Georgia nodded. "It made eight pounds this past month. It is not much, but it is a start and if I could only continue to write and publish more of my works, I could earn my own living! I do not have to be sent away! I can earn and help where I can here!"

"Eight pounds a month is not nearly enough to keep you," her mother replied.

Georgia stuttered for a second. "Yes, but if—if I could—If I were able to write more books, I would bring in more money."

"'If' is a beautiful dream, Georgia, but it is time for you to grow up," her mother replied coldly.

Evangelina made a noise, but whether it was a laugh or a huff, Georgia could not tell.

"You are determined to send me away then?" Georgia all but whispered.

"My dear," her mother began, "I hope you know I have no choice. With the circumstances being what they are, it is imperative that we take action now before it is too late. This is part of that action we have to take."

"Might I ask when you expect to have me sent away?" Georgia asked almost blandly.

"You will be twenty-three in a few months," her mother told her. "We will have found a family to place you in by then. I have already instructed your father to write to his brother-in-law to keep a look out for a nice family."

Georgia took in a shaky breath before letting it out slowly. "What if I marry?" she suggested. "Could I not help in that way? Could I not be taken care of by my husband?"

"My dear," her mother said gently, "as I have said, we are going to use your dowry to help pay off our debts.

"And what of Evangelina's dowry?" she pressed. "Are you going to use hers as well to wipe away our debts?"

Mrs. Hamilton cleared her throat. "Evangelina will need hers for when she marries and marries well, for she *is* expected to marry a man of great wealth."

Though his name was not mentioned, Georgia knew that man was Mr. Garret.

"Evangelina is expected to marry, but not me? I shall be written off without another thought? I, the *elder* sister, shipped away and forgotten?" She looked up at her father who blanched and turned away in shame.

"Without a dowry for you, there will be nothing to entice a man to marry you."

Georgia started, trying her best not to yell or glare at her mother. "Is that the only way you think a man will marry me? Is if you pay him? If you *buy* his love? Do I not have any good qualities of my own?"

Her mother did not reply.

Georgia looked up at her father again who finally dared to look at her, his facial expression desperately sullen. Though she could feel her heart shattering in her chest, she fought the urge to cry. She stood up straighter and took in slow deep breaths.

"Then it is decided," she said after a moment. "You both are in agreement?"

"It is for the best, my dear," her mother told her.

Georgia did not reply as she turned and left the room, rushing out of the front door and into the sun. She had just allowed a few of her bitter tears to fall when she saw a single rider coming up the road. It was Mr. Garret, their savoir, Evangelina's key to a life of luxury.

She swallowed her bitterness. It was not Mr. Garrett's fault they were in their predicament. She offered him a smile as he rode up to her.

"Good afternoon," she said, trying to put on the façade of cheerfulness.

"Good afternoon, Miss Hamilton. Are you for a walk?" he asked her, getting off his horse.

"I suppose I am," she replied. "My sister is in the parlor. It was good to see you again." She quickly curtseyed and turned to move away when he stopped her.

"Are you opposed to company?" he questioned.

"Are you offering your services?"

"I am," he replied. "But if you would much prefer to be alone, I would never dare to intrude upon your solitude."

"No," Georgia told him, her bitterness softening slightly. "I could use some company."

He bowed and handed his reins to a waiting servant before catching up to her.

"I do not want to seem impertinent," he said after a moment, "but it appears you are upset."

"Would it?" she replied a little more tetchily than she wanted. She sighed. "I apologize. I suppose I am a little."

"Might I be of some assistance? Perhaps talking about it could help."

Georgia laughed. "You have no idea how much assistance you already are," she retorted.

He seemed confused. "I beg your pardon?"

She shook her head. "Pay no mind to me," she said with a smile. "I am in a rare mood."

They broke off into silence for another moment or two.

"Can I ask you a question?" Mr. Garrett said.

"I do not know why you should not."

"Actually, I have asked it before, but the answer was interrupted. Why does everyone assume I am always here to visit your sister?"

She looked at him. "Because everyone comes to visit my sister," she told him plainly.

"Do you not receive any visitors of your own?"

She shrugged. "I used to. Louisa Barker, before she was married, visited often. As well as Sarah Marmouth, Patricia Hamm, Marcia Stuart, and Annabelle Leigh."

"And where are they all?"

"Married," Georgia replied hoping she did not sound as begrudgingly as she felt. "All of them married and moved away. Well, except poor Annabelle Leigh. She passed away two years ago."

"Does Mr. Fairgrove not visit you? I thought you were friends."

"Ross?" she asked, huffing. "Even he comes for Evangelina. So, *that* is how I know you are here for my sister, Mr. Garrett. They all are. I am used to it by now."

He shook his head. "It is a shame you feel that way."

"How do you mean?" she asked. "I do not feel anything about it. It is just a fact of life. My sister has all of the suitors while I have all of the friends who get married and leave."

"Do you not consider me your friend?" he asked her.

She regarded him for a moment.

"I thought we got along well enough," he pointed out. "We have a lot in common. We like the same books, neither of us seem to enjoy large gatherings, and we fall into conversation rather easily and comfortably. Say, for this one, perhaps."

Georgia smiled, warmed by his kindness, laughing lightly. "You are right, Mr. Garrett. Thank you for saying so. And, yes, I do consider you a friend."

"Good." He nodded. "Then you shall have at least one visitor that comes to see you."

"Mr. Garrett!" Evangelina's voice rang out somewhere behind them.

Mr. Garrett blushed at the sound of his name and turned to see Evangelina floating up to them. Georgia smiled softly despite her disappointment.

"Thank you for walking with me," she said to him. "But I think I shall prefer to walk a bit on my own."

"Miss Hamilton, wait," he replied. "I do not think you quite understand me."

"It is alright, Mr. Garrett," Georgia told him with a smile and without bitterness in her voice. "There is nothing to explain. I understand perfectly. I am only just the sister of the prettiest girl in the country."

"I did not know you were here, Mr. Garrett," Evangelina said a little breathlessly as she came upon them. "How devilish of you to sneak off without me, Georgia."

Georgia strained a smile onto her thin lips. "Indeed it was," she replied. "I am done, however. I wish to write Louisa a letter." She curtseyed. "Good day, Mr. Garrett."

"Good day, Miss Hamilton."

Georgia quickly moved past them, making her way to her room where she locked the door and sobbed.

9

A week had passed, and Georgia had yet to give up on her wish for happiness. She had received another letter from William Henry a few days after hers was sent that confirmed her belief that she was just as close at happiness as her sister was.

He told her of her many qualities, numerated everything he was in awe about her, and recollected the day he first saw her. Georgia had never felt so alive as when she read his letters to her. They were so full of feeling and dedication that she felt she should burst.

She wrote back to him, hurrying his arrival, pressing upon him her desire to meet him again.

The day my eyes look upon you again will be one of the happiest of my life, she wrote.

She wanted to tell him of her situation. She wanted to let him know that she was in danger of being sent away after her coming birthday, but she did not want her letters to be sent in desperation. She did not want her urgency toward being saved to overshadow the growing affection she had for him, and the affection she felt he returned with, perhaps, equal regard.

She merely noted that her wish to see him grew more every day and to wait another month seemed nearly impossible. *If there was anything I could do to return you sooner to me, if that were in my power to do so, I would have done it a thousand times over*, she said.

She truly hoped he would read her letter and flock to her and dreamed even more that he would make good on his promises and continue to be the man and lover he portrayed himself to be. She wished more than ever that he would come and whisk her away.

Georgia had to laugh at herself, though bitterly, at her change in attitude. It was not long since her sister put the image of a man running in the rain to save the woman he loved. The idea had been ridiculous at the time, but now it was all she wished for. To be saved.

Georgia maintained her bitter attitude around her family. She avoided anywhere her sister was going to be, tired of her taunts; she almost begrudgingly obeyed her mother when she 'needed' her; and she stopped visiting her father while he was in his study 'tending to business'.

No, she had already felt abandoned by them, more than she ever had before and, if her plans with William Henry did not pan out, she almost relished at the thought of moving away and never seeing them again. She was not good enough for them and, therefore, they were not good enough for her.

She made this sentiment very clear one day when she decided to visit Ross at his house. She caught him in the middle of writing a letter one morning not long after breakfast.

"Georgia," he said, almost surprised at seeing her. "What are you doing here?"

"Visiting," she replied matter-of-factly. "Do I disturb you?" She motioned her head to his writing desk.

"No," he told her with a soft smile. "It is something I can tend to later. Would you like to take a walk?"

Georgia shook her head. "No, but you can invite me to dinner," she informed him. "Which I will graciously accept."

"Dinner? We have only just broken our fast an hour or so ago."

"Oh, yes, then I suppose you shall have me for lunch as well."

He laughed. "Well, then, in that case, of course you are welcome."

She nodded her thanks as she sat down.

"Is something wrong?" Ross inquired after a moment, noticing the smile on her face fading.

Georgia sighed, creasing her brow. "Do you think I am nothing but a joke?"

"What?" Ross replied, confused. "What on earth are you talking about?"

Georgia laughed bitterly through her nose. "My family seems to think me so," she said softly. "They are shipping me off to some family after my twenty-third birthday."

Ross blinked in his confusion. "What?"

Georgia shook her head. "I am to be a governess."

Ross regarded her serious features and frowned. "What on earth?" He shook his head. "I do not understand. Why would they do such a thing?"

"We are broke, Ross," she confided. "My father has lost nearly everything in bad investments. Has spent all our money on faulty speculations! Our house has a mortgage that he cannot pay, and the bank is about ready to declare us bankrupt."

Ross gaped at her. "I cannot believe it," he mumbled.

"It is true. And I am to be sent off so I will no longer be a burden to my family. My dowry is to be spent paying off debts because even with my dowry, no man would ever want to marry me." Georgia did not visit Ross with the intention of crying, so she quickly composed herself and smiled. "So, I am off within a few months."

He shook his head, fumbling for something to say. "I cannot believe your father has allowed this."

"He said nothing when my mother demanded it of me."

"And Evangelina?" he asked hesitantly. "Are they sending her away too?"

Georgia stood angrily from her seat and moved to a window. "You know they would never," she answered a little bitterly. "She is the pretty daughter. The daughter they can have married off to a wealthy man. I am quite certain that man will be Mr. Garrett."

Ross's shoulders dropped. "Evangelina loves him then?"

Georgia laughed. "It is not about love at this point, Ross," she explained. "She has to marry for money so my father will not be completely ruined. If he loves her, that is all well and good, but my parents would not care a jot now regardless."

"What about your writing?" Ross asked. "Could that not maintain you? Tell them about your novel and your royalties!"

Georgia swallowed the lump in her throat. "I told them. Mother was horrified I was making money on my own before our situation was known. She said it would not make a difference." She shook her head. "But I am not deterred from writing. I will continue no matter what." Her lips twitched into a weak smile.

Ross smiled in return. "I would expect nothing less from you."

She took a deep breath and let it out slowly. "I did not mean to throw this on you."

He shook his head. "You are not throwing anything on me."

"You are just the only one I feel who would listen. My only friend, other than your sister, of course, but she is so far away."

"I know."

There was a brief silence between them.

"Do you remember William Henry from last summer?" she finally asked.

Ross looked up at her and nodded after a moment. "Yes, cousin of the Stanfords?"

Georgia nodded. "We have been writing back and forth," she confided with a smile. "I have not told my family."

Ross flashed his friend a sly smile. "Miss Georgia Hamilton, have you been keeping secrets?"

She smiled. "I suppose I have."

"How long has this been going on?"

"Almost a year," she told him, taking a moment to think. "It was completely unexpected. I just received a letter from him one day telling me he has not stopped thinking about me since we first met."

Ross raised his brows.

"He said he was too shy to approach me or say anything more to me than niceties," she continued.

Ross laughed through his nose. "Dear Georgia, I do believe you are blushing."

Georgia pressed her hand to her cheek and smiled. "I believe I am too."

"I am glad for it," he told her. "If anyone deserves to be happy, I am sure it is you."

She looked up at him with smirk. "*That* I do not think you believe at all," she laughed.

"Do you not?" he retorted. "I was not aware I had a habit of lying to you. As your friend, I think I have always told you the truth."

"Or told me what I have wanted to hear?"

He smiled but shook his head. "No, Georgie, not this time," he assured her. "This time, I mean it. You deserve happiness more than most."

Georgia sighed, relaxing a bit. "Thank you, Ross," she replied softly. "I am glad someone thinks so."

He stood and held out his arm for her. "Come," he told her. "Let us go and drink some canary and make fools of ourselves on the piano."

Georgia laughed. "Ross, it is only just after ten."

He shrugged. "Fine! Then we shall take a long walk around the grounds first."

"Then we shall play a few hands of whist?"

He groaned quietly. "Then we shall play a few hands of whist. But *then* we shall drink canary and I shall listen as you play horribly on the piano."

10

In the following days, the Hamilton family was invited to a gathering at the Lewis's house and in order to keep up appearances, everyone donned their finest evening wear and pretended to get along with one another. Georgia was still not talking to her parents other than to respond to their commands or questions in one-worded answers, but she was still expected to go. She refrained from groaning and instead made a point to be overly cheerful while in attendance.

Upon arriving at the Lewis's residence, she quickly sought out Ross who smiled kindly at her.

"I was thinking you would not come," he said handing her a glass of punch.

"Being too early are for those too eager to please," Georgia replied in a tone reflecting her mother. "If we arrive while most are already in attendance, then all eyes shall be on us."

Ross lifted a brow. "I shall keep that in mind," he huffed laughingly.

"Look at them parading themselves as if nothing is wrong," she almost mumbled watching her family float around the room smiling at their friends and acquaintances.

"They are keeping up an image," Ross replied.

"They are keeping up lies," she corrected.

"My, who is in a mood this evening?"

She sighed. "Forgive me," she told him. "There is one consolation. My father has not denied me my trip to visit your sister in September."

"I am glad for it. I know she misses you."

"Ross," Evangelina sang, gliding over to them. "You seemed to have taken extra care in your looks this evening."

Ross turned crimson. "I have done nothing different," he mumbled.

"Well, you look—you look decent," Evangelina told him in a

flat tone.

"Thank you," Ross replied slowly, a little confused. He exchanged looks with Georgia who shook her head, shrugging.

Evangelina looked as if she had something else to say to him but thought better of it.

"What do you need, Evangelina?" Georgia asked when her sister made no attempt to leave.

Evangelina cleared her throat. "Marcia Stuart is here and has been asking for you," she told Georgia.

Georgia's eyes lit up. "Is she?" she asked.

"She says she cannot stay long in her condition, so you better go and find her," Evangelina replied. She then shot another look at Ross before sashaying away.

Ross cleared his throat and shook his head. "Was that strange?"

"Yes, it was," Georgia said turning to him. "Honestly, I will never understand what you see in her. She is the wo—"

"Stop," he pleaded. "Please. I do not need to hear your disapproval of it. I feel what I feel and that is how it shall be."

Georgia regarded her friend for a moment. "Alright. I will respect that."

"Thank you."

"Well, I am going to find Marcia," she told him. "Will you join me?"

He shook his head. "I prefer to mope on my own."

"Now who is in a mood?"

He lifted a brow at her.

"Fine, but do not leave early," she ordered. "I expect at least one dance from you."

"Dance? There is no band to play."

Georgia laughed. "A house full of *accomplished* young ladies and you do not think the piano will be opened by any of them?"

He flashed her a smile. "You are right. If that happens, I will owe you a dance."

Georgia moved to look for her friend. She waded through the

small crowd, trying to squeeze her way through groups of people when someone, whose back was to her, took a step backwards and stepped on her foot.

The two nearly fell before catching their balance. Georgia looked up in the confusion to see Mr. Garrett, both of them flushing. A few of the guests laughing at the scene.

"Miss Hamilton," he said, embarrassment heightening his voice and flushing his cheeks. His eyes seemed to sparkle with the added color. "I do apologize. Have I hurt you?"

Georgia readjusted her glasses and pressed a hand to her chest, giving a small laugh. "Mr. Garrett, for a moment I thought we would fall over one another."

"I am sure if you were Evangelina, you would have," she heard someone say, causing a wave of laughter to course through the small circle of guests Mr. Garrett had just been talking to.

Georgia's smile fell from her face, but Mr. Garrett chose not to hear the comment. Instead, he extended his arm for her to take.

"Come, Miss Hamilton," he said with a grin. "You told me the last we met you had started reading *Frankenstein* and I am curious to know your feelings on it."

Georgia's smile returned to her face, appreciating the grace and good breeding Mr. Garrett portrayed as she slipped her arm through his. He led her to the other side of the room, finding a quiet corner set apart from the rest of the guests.

He sighed after a moment. "I am glad you have finally come," he told her. "I thought I would be forced to endure Mr. Lewis's obsequious civilities all evening."

Georgia laughed. "Yes, it seems he has been trying to press his daughter upon you," she replied.

"His attempts are certainly in vain. Miss Lewis is a nice girl, but she is not for me."

Georgia laughed again. "I think what you mean to say is Miss Veronica Lewis is *not* a nice girl, and, therefore, is not for you."

He suppressed a laugh. "At any rate, I am growing rather exhausted with all of these gatherings and balls. Are they always so frequent here?"

"Well, it is the season when handsome, rich, single men tend to visit the county, so you can bet they are not done with you yet."

He laughed. "Finally, some real honesty."

"I hope you can handle it. My mother often tells me I am too honest, and I should learn to hold my tongue, but being a rebellious sort, I do not see the fun in that."

"Good. I prefer you that way."

Georgia felt herself blush though she was not sure why.

"Now, *Frankenstein*," Mr. Garrett urged. "Tell me what you thought."

"Wonderfully tragic," she replied. "If I am honest, which we both know I am, I feel sorry for the wretch. He was such a pitiable creature."

"You feel bad for the monster?"

"Of course! It was not his fault he was the way he was. Victor Frankenstein created him and then left him to his own devices. He left this poor, scared creature out into the world unfeelingly. "

"But the monster killed several people."

"To protect himself, he did," Georgia argued lightly. "He was so misunderstood that people feared him and then they attacked him. What was he to do? All he wanted was to be understood and loved. Something his creator denied him."

Mr. Garrett nodded. "I see your argument. But that fear later turned to anger and he killed for vengeance."

"Well, yes, at that point, I began to pity him less."

"Georgia, is that you?"

Georgia turned to see Marcia Stuart walking over to her, her belly swollen with child. She beamed at her friend and embraced her. "Marcia! It is so good to see you!"

"I have been looking for you for some time," Marcia replied. "I sent your sister to fetch you."

Georgia pressed her hand to her cheek. "Forgive me, yes! I was on my way to look for you when I was distracted. Mr. Garrett reeled me in by talking of books." She held out her hand to Mr. Garrett. "Have you two met?"

Mr. Garrett bowed to her. "It is a pleasure, Mrs. Stuart," he said. "Miss Hamilton has told me good things about you."

Marcia regarded the two of them for a moment, a look of subtle suspicion on her face. "It is a pleasure meeting you as well, sir. I would curtsey, but it is less easy these days." She rubbed her round belly.

"Oh, I am so excited for you and your husband!" Georgia exclaimed. "You seem to be glowing."

"I do not feel that way," she replied. "I feel, well, rather large."

"I should leave the two of you to talk," Mr. Garrett said, not wanting to get in the way of their conversation.

"Nonsense, Mr. Garrett," Marica told him. "I shall not stay long. Besides, I very rudely interrupted your conversation just so I could selfishly see my friend for a few moments. I would not wish to get between the two of you."

Georgia furrowed her brows in confusion at her friend's statement, while Mr. Garrett nodded his thanks.

"When are you due?" Georgia asked after a moment.

"In two months, or so the doctor says."

Georgia quietly gasped. "Perhaps we will share a birthday! What a wonderful present that should be!"

Marcia smiled at her friend, reaching out to squeeze her hand. "I make no promises, but I shall try my best." She squeezed her hand again.

"How is living in London?" Georgia asked her. "Do you see as many plays as you thought you would?"

"Jonathan and his family have a box, so I can catch a show here and there. We live near the park, too. It is so beautiful in the spring! I must have you for a visit. I would love to see your witticisms up against the over-serious Londoners."

"Miss Hamilton would certainly give them something to talk about," Mr. Garrett interjected with a smile.

"Would I?" Georgia almost laughed. "I have been to London on numerous occasions and doubt I have ever left being so popular."

Mr. Garrett chuckled. "You do not think you have ever stirred the mind of some self-important gentleman always thinking he is due gratification?"

Georgia laughed and looked at Marcia. "What in the world is he saying, Marcia? He would have you think I am some philosopher had you not known me better."

Marcia smiled, glancing between them. "Perhaps not a philosopher, Georgia, but a cynic."

She grinned at her friend. "What a friend you are. That is hardly better!"

Mr. Garrett chuckled again. "I was referring to neither. I was simply alluding to the fact that you make some surprisingly deep conversations on occasion. Conversations that would make anyone, including the self-absorbed Londoner, think twice about certain subjects. It gives you a sense of mysteriousness."

Georgia pressed her hand to her mouth to stifle another laugh. "I have never in my life been called such a thing. What say you, Marcia? Do you find me mysterious?"

Marcia tilted her head slightly, her hand absent-mindedly rubbing her belly. "Yes, I can see there is a sense of mysticism about you. Though I think I would be more apt to call you surprising than mysterious as you often say things that are unexpected."

Georgia pressed her lips together as she smiled. "I think I like this caricature of my character. Thank you both for the lovely sketch of it."

"Yes, but what was mysterious was a certain book I read by a certain Lady H," Marcia continued grinning at her friend.

Georgia turned crimson, becoming speechless.

"You have read *The Winds of Westbrook*?" Mr. Garrett asked. "I read it not too long ago. It was very well written."

Marcia gaped smilingly at Mr. Garrett.

"I have recommended it to Miss Hamilton, but I do not believe she has looked into it yet."

Marcia pressed her lips together and glanced between her friend and Mr. Garrett. "If I am not mistaken—"

Georgia's eyes grew wide as she saw the mischief flashing in her friend's.

"—Georgia was the first person to read *The Winds of Westbrook.*"

Mr. Garrett creased his brow. "Is that so?"

Marcia nodded. "Georgia knows Lady H personally—intimately, you might say."

Georgia pursed her lips and closed her eyes.

Mr. Garrett looked at Georgia for several moments before the realization dawned on him. "*You* are Lady H?" he asked in a surprised whisper.

Georgia gave a single nod and sighed. "I am."

Mr. Garrett chuckled. "That is amazing!" He gestured to her with his hands. "You are amazing! I cannot believe you did not tell me sooner."

"It was supposed to be a secret," Georgia replied, shooting her friend an accusing look.

Marcia laughed and rubbed her friend's arm. "I wish I could stay longer, but I must be going," she told them. "I grow more exhausted by the day." She smiled at Mr. Garrett. "It was a pleasure meeting you, sir. Do take care of my friend. She is one of the best people I know."

"You should come over for tea, Marcia," Georgia urged. "There is so much to catch up on."

"Unfortunately, we leave tomorrow," Marcia told her. "We spent a few weeks in Brighton and only stopped for a night before returning home. We were not going to but I begged Jonathan so I could see my friends again." She regarded Mr. Garrett again, looking at him looking at Georgia. "You should visit soon."

Georgia nodded. "I wish to."

They said their goodbyes again and Georgia watched as her friend left.

"She seems very kind," Mr. Garrett said.

"For once," Georgia began, "you are actually right when you say 'kind.'" She smirked at him. "Marcia was always wonderful. She shall be a good mother."

"I cannot believe you are Lady H!" Mr. Garrett began again. "I mean, I *can* believe it, but I am still in awe that it is you." He shook his head, smiling. "You let me talk about how much I enjoyed your book without saying a word."

"I am not one to boast, but I am sure you could have talked more about how wonderful it is."

He laughed. "You do surprise, Miss Hamilton."

They continued their conversation about her book and her dreams of continuing to write as they laughed and joked. Guests observed them from other parts of the room, questioning to themselves and others why Mr. Garrett was spending so much time with plain Georgia Hamilton. What could they be talking about that was interesting enough to keep him from Evangelina?

Further into the evening, with Mr. Garrett and Georgia still off in the corner by themselves, a few of the young ladies decided there must be dancing and the piano was soon opened. Georgia looked up from their conversation to see Anne Fitch taking her turn at the piano first. She then noticed the small group of couples standing up waiting to dance.

She frowned when she saw Mr. Talbot standing up with Jennifer Hayes. From the look on her sister's face, Georgia could tell she wasn't happy.

"Would you like to dance?" he asked her.

"I would not mind it so much," she replied. "Though I did make a bet with Ross that if the piano was opened up, he was to dance with me. And it seems as though he very begrudgingly is making good on that bet."

They both laughed as they saw the somewhat put out Ross making his way toward them.

"My sister, however, does seem without a partner," Georgia told him.

He nodded. "Then I will be happy to oblige."

"I suppose you are over here gloating at being right?" Ross huffed, holding out his hand to Georgia.

She smirked at Mr. Garrett as she took Ross's hand. "What on earth would give you that impression?"

Once the dance was started, order seemed to return as Mr. Garrett, the most handsome man in the room, stood up with Evangelina Hamilton, the prettiest girl. It was as if the whole gathering breathed a sigh of relief, letting out their confusion as to why Mr. Garrett and the less attractive Hamilton sister seemed to be in each other's confidence.

It was, of course, because Miss Georgia Hamilton, often has too much to say and Mr. Garrett is too nice to interrupt anyone when speaking, and, therefore, only listened so as not to offend the sister of his future wife.

It could not be denied; Mr. Garrett and Evangelina made the most beautiful couple. It only made sense that they should be together. And it was with extreme luck that Mr. Garrett was as nice as he was.

During the dance, however, Georgia made a few observations of her own. Jennifer and Mr. Talbot seemed to be on friendlier terms than she had last surmised. She watched as their eyes never left one another and she observed that Evangelina noticed it too. She watched as her sister's smile fell a few times as she saw her friend and Mr. Talbot flirt.

After several minutes of this uncomfortableness, Evangelina forced a smile on her face and began flirting with Mr. Garrett. She commented on his hair and choice of cravat, often laughing at his remarks.

If this was not enough, Ross, who had also been watching Evangelina had a frown on his face, making him a poor partner. The tension on the dancefloor was almost palpable and Georgia was relieved when the song was finally over.

Mr. Garrett looked as if he were to move in Georgia's direction when Evangelina looped her arm in his.

"Come, Mr. Garrett," she said. "Let us take a walk outside. It is rather stuffy in here. Do you not agree?"

Mr. Garrett stammered for a moment. "Y-yes, I, uh, I suppose it is," he replied.

"You want a drink?" Ross asked Georgia, bringing her attention back to him.

She turned to him. "Absolutely." She followed him through the next round of couples waiting to dance.

On their way to grab a drink, Georgia's mother stopped her by taking her by the arm. She pulled her eldest daughter aside out of earshot of the other guests.

"What were you doing earlier talking so long with Mr. Garrett?" she asked her.

Georgia gave her mother a shocked look. "We were doing just that, mamma," she replied. "Talking."

"It is not for you to talk to Mr. Garrett for so long," she scolded her. "He is for Evangelina, not you."

"He is my friend," Georgia told her a little defiantly. "I was not aware I was forbidden from having friends."

"Do not take Mr. Garrett's kindness as friendship, Georgia. Nor should you think to bore him with your chatter."

Georgia took in a sharp breath.

"We need Mr. Garrett to spend as much time as possible with your sister," her mother continued. "He should not be idling away his time with you."

Georgia glared at her mother. "You are right, mamma," she replied ripping her arm out of her mother's grasp. "I forgot I am nothing but an embarrassment to you."

"Oh, there is no need to be dramatic, Georgia," her mother said taking a champagne flute from a tray as a servant walked by.

"Am I being dramatic, mamma?" Georgia challenged. "I am the daughter you are robbing of her dowry and shipping off to take care of another family's children. You are hiding me away!"

"Keep your voice down," Mrs. Hamilton whispered. "And I am not hiding you away. I am sending you away so that you will be taken care of."

Georgia scoffed. "Forgive me if I do not believe you, mamma." She then walked away, rushing to catch up with Ross.

He handed her a punch upon seeing her. "What was that about?" he asked her.

Georgia refrained from huffing. "Just a few words of encouragement from my loving mother," she replied with a forced smile.

"Should I have grabbed you a brandy instead of the punch?"

She laughed through her nose. "Perhaps. Then maybe I can get drunk and play the piano horribly in front of all of our neighbors and really give my mother a reason to want to ship me off."

"I will marry you myself if you pulled that off."

Georgia pressed a hand to her mouth to suppress a chuckle. "Yes, and then we both can be miserable."

"Is that not what we are now?"

Georgia looked at him. "Yes, but why do we have to be? What is stopping either of us from being happy?"

"Life finds a way to make everyone miserable at one time or another, I suppose," Ross replied taking a sip from his drink.

"How convenient."

Not long after, Evangelina and Mr. Garrett returned from their walk, it being interrupted by a steady sprinkle of rain. Seeing Georgia and Ross, he made his way over to them, his hair slightly damp and scattered about his forehead.

On anyone else, the effect would make them look disheveled and unkempt, but on Mr. Garrett, it only seemed to enhance his high cheeks bones and glowing skin. Georgia had to clear her throat as he tossed his head in a motion to flip his hair out of his eyes.

"Rain caught you by surprise then?" Ross asked with a grin.

"Quite," Mr. Garrett replied pulling out his handkerchief and patting his face dry.

"Where did my sister go?" Georgia asked, looking away. She scanned the room, searching for her when she caught her sneaking out the door into another hallway.

"I am not sure," Mr. Garrett replied. "She said she had to find a towel."

"Will you excuse me?" she asked, handing what was left of her drink to Ross and pushing her way in the direction she saw her sister go. She pushed through the door exiting the large room. She stood for a moment in the hallway, looking left and right as she tried to figure out which way her sister went when she heard voices around the corner. She crept slowly in their direction, careful not to make a sound, stopping once the voices became clearer.

"Why does it matter with whom I dance?" came the indifferent voice of Mr. Talbot.

"You had promised to dance with me," replied Evangelina.

"Did I?" Mr. Talbot questioned. "I do not remember making such a promise. Besides, you seemed to have done just fine with your actual partner. Mr. Garrett is well sought after, is he not?"

Georgia thought she could detect a sneer in his voice.

Evangelina sighed deeply. "I do not care for him," she confessed, a hint of desperation in her voice. "I care for you."

Georgia's eyes grew wide, and she pressed her hand to her mouth to keep from gasping.

"I do not believe it," Mr. Talbot told her. "I have seen you flirting with him."

"As I have seen you flirting with Jennifer Hayes!" she retorted angrily. "Are you to tell me you have feelings for her?"

"I might."

Evangelina huffed. "You are a liar," she said a little heatedly. "You do not care one jot for her just as I do not care one jot for Mr. Garrett."

Mr. Talbot laughed through his nose. "Oh, yes, I am sure you do not. Run along, little Evangelina. I am sure you are missed."

Georgia heard the sound of footsteps and slipped into another room just before Mr. Talbot rounded the corner. She then waited for another minute before peering back out into the hall where the sounds of muffled sobs could be heard.

She slowly walked down the hall, turning the corner to see her sister with her face buried in her hands. She felt for her deeply and reached out to put a gentle hand on her shoulder which caused Evangelina to jump.

"It is only me," Georgia told her in a soft voice.

"What do you want?" her sister sniffled back, her hair slightly flattened from the rain.

"I came to see if you were alright."

Evangelina huffed. I am sure that is exactly what you came to do." She pulled out a handkerchief and dabbed at her eyes. "I am fine, however."

Georgia shook her head. "You do not have to put on a brave face with me, Lina," she told her tenderly. "I am your sister. If something is wrong, you can tell me."

Evangelina paused, staring at her sister before letting out a small laugh. "To what purpose would that serve?" she retorted.

"I can help you with your problems; share your burdens; keep your secrets," Georgia explained. "I can help you lighten your load."

Evangelina laughed again. "You make yourself sound like a pack-mule," she replied. She sniffed and wiped her nose on her handkerchief before pinching her cheeks and straightening her back. "At any rate, I do not need help from you. Especially since nothing is wrong." She pushed past her sister and walked back in the direction of the party.

Georgia followed her with a heavy heart.

"Where did you run off to?" Ross asked when she returned.

Georgia sighed. "Nowhere important." She looked around. "Where is Mr. Garrett?"

"Your sister stole him away just a minute ago," Ross tried not to grumble.

She turned and caught sight of them from across the room. For a moment her eyes locked with Mr. Garrett's, and she thought she perceived a smile, but it was short lived as a few more of the young women in attendance quickly surrounded him.

Georgia laughed at the sight, but internally her stomach was in knots.

11

It was almost July and Georgia, who had not received a reply to her last letter in almost two weeks, was sullen. Her family thought her mood was an extension of their conversation weeks prior, and had no suspicion of her hopes of being saved by a man to whom she had been writing.

Her father, often shooting her guilty looks, tried more than once to engage her into conversation, but she was not inclined to reciprocate his attentions. She had felt abandoned by him and was not yet ready to forgive.

More than anyone, Georgia avoided her sister, whose snide remarks had grown in viciousness. Her mother was another story. Their relationship did not much differ as she never seemed to be of much consequence to her before and was less so after she decided to have her sent away.

Through all of this, Georgia tried to remain positive. She tried to visit Ross as often as she could and even wished Mr. Garrett was around to visit her. She had been disappointed when she, surprisingly, received a letter from him saying he had to rush home to Cornwall to take care of business.

"Why should he write to you and not Evangelina?" her mother had questioned her.

"I do not know, mamma," Georgia replied a little exasperatedly. "He says he shall return in a couple weeks' time. You can ask him then."

Her mother had huffed at this, complaining that he should have stopped by and made his sentiments known before he left. "He should have at least spoken to Evangelina," she continued. "To just leave her wondering in the wind about his affections is rather ungentlemanly if you ask me."

Evangelina seemed less worried about the sudden departure of

Mr. Garrett than anyone. She still made sure to attend every ball and gathering she was invited to, especially if Mr. Talbott would be in attendance. *Particularly* if Mr. Talbot was in attendance.

Georgia noticed this and tried, once again, to urge her against the evils of such a man, but Evangelina always laughed her off.

"I am not serious about Mr. Talbot," she told her. "He is just a small flirtation. Completely harmless."

"It is often the harmless flirtations that do one the most harm," she warned to no avail.

Evangelina merely laughed. "Really, Georgie! Mr. Talbot is a nobody."

Georgia, though she did not believe her sister, did not press her any further and, therefore, dropped the subject completely.

Finally, the day came when Georgia had a reply from William Henry. Her heart stopped in her throat as she took the letter and walked briskly to her spot under the oak tree. She then tore apart the seal and opened the letter, greedily taking in its contents.

She sighed a breath of relief when she saw his late reply was due to him traveling and foolishly forgetting to leave a forwarding address for his mail. The rest gave way to brighten her hopes as he revealed to her that he was to visit his cousins the following week.

Georgia's breath caught in her throat and her eyes watered as she thought of meeting with the man on which so many of her hopes hung. The man who had already confessed his feelings for her, who now vowed to spend every waking moment he could by her side.

There was no need for her to write a response, as by the time he received one he would already be on his way. She was to expect him the following Monday.

The next several days saw Georgia in a brighter mood as she moved about the house with a smile on her face. It was such a change from how she had been acting as of late that everyone in the house seemed to comment on it. Even a few of the servants whispered amongst themselves the change in not only her attitude, but her appearance.

Georgia seemed to take more interest in her dress and hair than before, spending longer than was usual at her vanity. She would ask her maid to try several different hairstyles on her, asking for ornaments like feathers or flowers to adorn them.

Her father, watching her stroll down the hall past his study one day, stopped her and asked her to come in. She hesitated at first but did as she was bid.

"Georgia," he began slowly, "I wish you would talk to me."

She pursed her lips for a moment. "I am not sure what there is to say, papa," she replied. "Everything has already been said for me."

He nodded. "This is not what I want for you, you know," he told her softly. "I have only ever wished for your happiness."

Georgia let out a sigh. "I know, papa," she replied. "But what I would have wished from you, is for you to have stood up for me."

Her father looked ashamed. "As I should have."

Georgia did not reply.

After several long moments, he nodded. "Then I shall."

Georgia furrowed her brow at him. "What do you mean?"

"I shall talk to your mother," he clarified. "If you do not wish to become a governess, we should not force you."

"Do you mean it?"

He smiled at her. "If you wish to continue to write and have a thousand more of your books published, I will not stand in your way."

Georgia's eyes welled up with tears. "Thank you, papa," she replied rushing to kiss him.

He patted her shoulder. "There is no need for tears," he told her. "I will figure something out for us all."

She wiped her eyes, half laughing. "I will give you all that I earn to help pay for me or to go toward whatever is needed."

He took her hand and patted it. "No, you will keep what you earn."

Georgia gaped at her father. "But, papa, we need the money, and every bit helps."

He shook his head. "This is a mess I created, and *I* will find a way to remedy it without taking from my children."

"I would be happy to help, papa!"

He kissed her hand. "I know, my dear. But my pride will not allow it." He pulled her in for another embrace, kissing the top of her forehead. "I do not deserve you."

"You do not have to tell mother right away if you would rather not," she said after a moment, pulling away. "Give yourself a few days to prepare."

He smiled at her. "You are always thinking of others," he replied with a nod. He then creased his brow as he noticed her hair. "What is all this?" He gingerly reached out and fingered the feather sticking from her head.

Georgia blushed, clearing her throat. "I have heard it is the fashion."

Mr. Hamilton huffed laughingly. "The fashion?" he repeated, trying not to laugh. "Since when did you care about such things?"

Georgia felt a little silly as she shrugged, straightening her glasses. "I do not care really. I was just trying it to see if I liked it, or maybe it suited me."

Mr. Hamilton cupped his daughter's cheek. "You do not need dressing up to light up someone's world, my dear. You are your own light."

Georgia smiled and kissed her father's hand.

"Yes, yes, child," he said lovingly. "Now, run along and order me some tea."

She planted another kiss on his cheek before she rushed out of the room with another reason to be happy.

12

Monday soon came and Georgia could hardly contain herself. She took extra care in getting ready, fidgeting the entire morning.

"Are you unwell?" her sister commented, not out of any concern but confusion by her sister's odd behavior.

"Very well, thank you," Georgia replied without a fuss.

Georgia rejoiced even more when her mother and sister accepted invitations to tea at the Lewis's, leaving her practically alone to receive William when he finally came. She eagerly watched the two of them go, waving gleefully as the carriage pulled away.

She then went up to her room and retouched her hair before pacing anxiously. Just before four, he arrived. A servant knocked on the door to her room to announce her visitor causing her to flush almost in a panic.

"I shall be down shortly," she replied without breathing. She stood in front of her mirror and smoothed her dress, trying to wipe the sweat from her palms at the same time. When she thought herself composed enough, she took a deep breath and strolled down the stairs.

Georgia paused for a moment, her hands shaking slightly as she opened the door to the parlor. She then burst into the room, her heart overflowing with more happiness than she had ever known.

"William!" she exclaimed seeing the average-looking man about average height glancing anxiously about the room.

The young man's features brightened at the sound of his name but were soon replaced by a look of confusion upon seeing Georgia.

Not noticing, however, she took William's hands in hers and pressed them gently. "You do not know how long I have waited for this moment," she told him. "I secretly hoped, wished that this would happen, but I never dreamed it would. You could never understand how happy you have made me."

The man before her blinked, unsure what to do.

"And now you have come!" Georgia continued almost breathlessly. "Have you just arrived in town? Are you settled at your cousins' house? You must sit and tell me of your travels!"

William stuttered for a moment. "I, uh, I am so sorry. Who are you?" he finally asked after a tense-filled moment.

Georgia gaped at him, unable to reply for several seconds. "Georgia," she finally told him quietly. "I am Georgia."

"Oh, no," William replied with a shake of his head, taking his hands back slowly. "Georgia is- she is supposed to be—" He cleared his throat. "I believe I have made a mistake," he finally choked out. "I thought I was talking to—"

"My sister," Georgia said once the realization hit her. Her heart sunk, and her knees felt weak. She released a shaky huff, everything inside of her seeming to shatter. "You thought I was Evangelina," she whispered. "You mixed up our names."

There was a brief awkward silence where Georgia felt her heart being torn into several pieces. She turned from William and closed her eyes, suppressing a groan.

"I am terribly sorry for the mix up," William told her, a twisted look of embarrassed confusion on his face. "I truly thought—"

"So is that it then?" Georgia interrupted, turning back to him, a blind rage coursing through her. "After all of our letters, our conversations, everything we have shared! A year of being each other's confidantes, waiting eagerly for the next letter. All of that means nothing because you realized you were talking to me and not my sister?"

"Of course, it does not mean 'nothing,'" he replied hesitantly. "What I said in those letters, I meant."

"But what you said was meant for my sister."

William looked uncomfortable.

"You might have begun with the perception that you were talking to my sister, but it was me who replied. It was my words that excited you, was it not?" She scanned his face as she tried to find the answer she was hoping for. "You began with the notion that you cared for my sister, but it was *my* words, *my* character—it was *me* with whom you really connected! Evangelina is none of those things. All of the good qualities you praised me on were mine alone!" Georgia could feel her breaths coming in shakily and she blinked back her tears before they could fall.

William, however, appeared unmoved by her plight, shifting comfortably and averting his eyes.

"That *is* it, then?" she said once she realized her attempts to sway him were in vain. The past year of hopeful and happy correspondence evaporated before her.

William cleared his throat then swallowed. "Well, I thought- perhaps, we might still be," he paused, "friends," he finally said, elongating the word.

"Get out of my house," Georgia told him sternly without hesitation.

"I beg your pardon?"

"Get out of my house!" she repeated louder.

William jumped at the anger in her voice. "That is a little sudden," he replied defensively. "After I came all of this way, I should at least be able to meet with your sister."

Georgia screamed in frustration and moved to the door, motioning to their butler waiting just outside the room.

"Remove this man!" she ordered. "He is an imposter, a fraud, a- a- an odious man and I never want to see him again!"

Georgia, who was not one for outbursts, especially ones of extreme anger, was taken seriously and her butler promptly escorted the disappointed man out of the house.

"This is unheard of! I have been misled in the most upsetting way!" he was heard shouting as he was led out.

Georgia waited until their footsteps faded before she pressed a hand to her stomach and released an anguished sob. How could she ever think that anyone would ever feel for her the way he had portrayed in his letters? Stupid, ignorant, silly girl! She had let a ridiculous fancy run away with her and it had left her with nothing but feelings of shame and torment.

She shook her head at her mistake.

"Never again," she said through her tears. "Never again will I be fooled by beautiful words."

It was in this state of mind that Mr. Garrett found her not half an hour later, her eyes red and puffy from crying, and her wit sharp and ready.

"Miss Hamilton," Mr. Garrett beamed as he walked into the room, a parcel in his hands.

She turned to look at him, his eyes seeming to glow as they saw her, but only for a second as they took in her features.

"Mr. Garrett," she said almost blandly, "you have returned rather soon from your business."

He cleared his throat and shook his head. "Yes, the business was not as extensive as I thought it would be," he replied, his brows furrowed in confusion as he looked at her.

Georgia nodded.

"Forgive me," he began, cautiously, "has something happened? Are you unwell?"

"Why should you think that?"

Mr. Garrett looked unsure as to what he should say. "I mean no disrespect, nor do I wish to be impertinent, but it appears as if you have been crying." His voice was level and showed genuine concern, but Georgia was in no mood for pity.

"I suppose I have," she replied a little tartly. "It seems I have suffered a small disappointment."

Mr. Garrett waited for her to continue, but when she didn't, he felt the need to say something himself. "Is it something I might be of assistance with?"

Georgia gave a small laugh. "Oh, Mr. Garrett, what could you know of disappointment?" she asked challengingly. "What in your life has ever been so disagreeable that you have been reduced to a burden in the eyes of your family?"

Mr. Garrett frowned. "Your tone implies that I never have, so I assume that is your belief?"

Georgia shook her head. "What could a man of considerable fortune and handsome features ever know of disappointment? Of heartbreak?"

Mr. Garrett looked offended. "You think money and good looks save you from such things?" he retorted.

"I do."

"What a bitter view of the world you have," he replied.

"I told you as much when we met," she returned blandly.

"Yes, but I did not think you so shallow as well."

Georgia took in an angry breath through her nose. "What do you know of it?" she asked heatedly. "You who is fawned over by pretty girls just wishing for you to look their way, to show them attention. You who parades into our town and has every ear perked in your direction, waiting for you to say something to them, to notice them."

Mr. Garrett shook his head. "Have I missed something?" he said, bewildered. "What has brought about this argument? Have I said or done something to offend you?"

In fact, he had not. Georgia was not directly angry at Mr. Garrett, but at William Henry and the world. More specifically, she was angry at herself for so easily being taken in. Mr. Garrett, who truly was just an innocent party in all of this, represented everything she will never have.

Despite this and because of it, Georgia gave Mr. Garrett a defiant look. "I am below everyone's notice, Mr. Garrett," she replied haughtily. "There is no reason to think I can be offended."

His frown deepened. "I am very sorry to say that I have been wrong about you, Miss Hamilton," he told her. "If that is not the case, then something has happened for you to change for the worse in the four weeks I have been gone. I left with us as friends only to return to your disdainful behavior toward me."

Georgia did not reply.

"Tell me, what has happened for I am at an utter loss," he seemed to plead. "Tell me I was not wrong about you."

Georgia shifted her gaze to the floor. "It is best, Mr. Garrett," she replied slowly, "that you continue to court my sister without my interference. I am for no one as I hold disdain for everyone."

Mr. Garrett looked at her in disappointment. "I wonder where your confidence has gone," he said softly. "I am sorry you have lost it." He placed the parcel he had been holding on a side table. "I shall heed your advice, however. Good day, Miss Hamilton."

He bowed to her and left.

Georgia blinked after him, taking a deep shaky breath as the sound of his footsteps faded down the hall. When she was sure he had gone, her gaze drifted to the parcel. She stared at it for a moment before she walked over and picked it up, slowly unwrapping it.

She let out a sigh when she saw the most beautiful journal she had ever seen. She placed her hand on the smooth leather of the binding and fingered the gold-foil impression of a bird in flight on the front. After several moments of admiring it, she opened the journal, listening to the creaking of the unused leather as she did so.

She shook her head and huffed when she read a small note scrawled in Mr. Garrett's hand: *May the words written in this journal be the key to the door you are looking for.*

An overwhelming feeling of guilt and shame came over her as she looked at it. How could she have been so hateful toward him when all he had ever been was kind? She took in a deep breath and let it out slowly.

It was too late now to regret what she never truly possessed.

GEORGIA APPROACHED HER FATHER LATER THAT EVENING FINDING HIM with his feet propped up on his desk and a book in his hand. He looked up, however, upon hearing her and smiled.

"Hello, my dear," he said putting his book away and motioning her to join him. "Have you come to challenge me in a game of backgammon?"

Georgia smiled weakly at him. "No, papa," she replied softly. "I have come to tell you that I accept."

He blinked at her in confusion. "Accept?" he repeated. "What on earth are you talking about?"

"I will become a governess," she told him. "I will not fight you on it. I will give up my rights to my dowry and resign myself to a life of serving others."

Her father frowned at her. "What nonsense is this? Was it not just the other day that we decided you would not do this?"

Georgia sniffed and nodded. "Yes, but it does not matter now." She shifted her gaze to the floor.

Her father stood and walked over to her, taking her gently by the chin and making her look at him. "What is the matter, Georgia?" he asked, his voice full of concern.

"If it is all the same to you, papa, I would much rather not talk about it."

Her father shook his head. "It is not all the same," he replied. "Something has happened, and I would like to know what it is."

Georgia blushed and turned her head. "I thought I was in love," she began. "And what is worse, I thought he was in love too." She shut her eyes and shook her head. "But I was wrong. It was just a silly fancy. I know that now."

Mr. Hamilton pulled his daughter in for a hug and kissed the top of her head. "I am sorry, my child, that you had to experience something like that, but one failed attempt at love does not mean you should give up forever."

Georgia took a step back from her father. "But look at me!" she exclaimed. "I am not pretty or graceful or elegant." She shook her head. "I am plain and uninteresting! I am nothing that a man wants for a wife! And now I shall have no dowry to entice a man, for that is the only way I could! If I were rich!"

"I will hear none of that!" her father protested, a little hurt at her indirect accusation.

"Papa," Georgia said, looking at him earnestly. "You know it to be true."

After a moment, Mr. Hamilton took a deep breath and let it out slowly. "I am sure to some you seem plain and a little opinionated."

Georgia gave him a look.

"Just let me finish," he said holding up a hand in defense. "I am sure to some, they look at you and see an unextraordinary girl with less than an awe-inspiring appearance, but that is not what I see when I look at you." He placed a hand on her cheek. "To me, you are a ray of sunshine in a dark room; you are an intelligent word in a conversation of stupidity; you are a fit of laughter on a dull evening." He brushed back a lock of her hair. "Others might only see what you look like, but I see who you are and that is more beautiful than anything or anyone I have ever met."

Georgia quickly wiped away a tear. "But that is not what men want. I am not what men want."

He shook his head. "You are what some men have yet to realize they want," he corrected. "Beauty fades, my dear. But wit and humor do not."

Georgia buried her head into her father's chest and cried.

"Hush now, child," he cooed. "Do not make decisions based on broken hearts. We shall see how you are feeling in a week or two and we shall go from there."

Georgia nodded. "Thank you, papa," she whispered.

"Now, can I still convince you to play me in a game of backgammon?" he asked. "You are still up by two games, and I am feeling rather lucky tonight."

Georgia laughed and wiped her face with the handkerchief her father held out for her. She nodded. "Do not think I shall show you any pity just because you said a few kind words just now." She smirked.

Her father smiled back. "I was thinking no such thing."

13

The weeks went by, and more gatherings and balls were held throughout the neighborhood because what else did the rich have to do but enjoy themselves? Work was left for the lower classes, and business usually only meant the sending of a few letters or lackadaisically checking on their investments from time to time. Therefore, gatherings and balls had to be held to pass their time lest they drown in an overwhelming sense of ennui. This forced Georgia out into the society that had rejected her more than once. Despite all of that, she was determined to put a smile on her face and pretend to not be miserable like everyone else.

"I am sorry, but have we met?" Ross asked her when she walked over to him one evening at the Dorsets'.

She lifted a brow at him.

"You are actually smiling," he pointed out. "I almost did not recognize you."

"Is it convincing then?" she asked taking the drink he proffered her.

"No more than anyone else's."

There was a loud fit of laughter from the other side of the room, and they turned to see William Henry with a group of other young men talking. Georgia huffed.

"I am sorry for that," he told her.

"For what?"

"For the situation with William Henry," he clarified. "I know that must not have been easy."

Georgia sipped her drink. "I should have known to begin with he wanted Evangelina," she grumbled. "It is my own fault really."

"Would you stop that!" Ross said in a stern tone. "I will have no more of your pity parties. What happened was awful, but it is not your fault for feeling for someone. He is the idiot in this equation."

"How so?"

"For one, he is not even smart enough to remember the name of the girl he is trying to woo," Ross pointed out. "Secondly, despite having fallen for you in your letters, with you having poured your soul into them, he still could not see the beauty that you are."

Georgia groaned.

"I mean it, Georgia," he told her. "You are a wonderful person, full of life and spirit."

"Yes, yes, please tell me how a real man will not love me for how plain I look but because I can tell a joke and make him laugh. It is my wit that weighs my worth, not my lackluster looks," Georgia replied begrudgingly. "It would be nice coming from someone else other than my father."

"I beg your pardon, but did I not just say that?" Ross asked, his brow arched.

"Oh, you are no better," she replied, waving her hand dismissively. "You are more a brother to me than anyone. Of course, you would say those things.

Ross shrugged. "Well, if you do not want to be comforted, I will not waste my breath." His eyes caught sight of Mr. Garrett whispering into Evangelina's ear and he blushed. "You know, until recently, I would have said Mr. Garrett preferred you over your sister."

Georgia laughed. "That would be a world out of balance, would it not?"

"I mean it," he told her. "He seemed to gravitate toward you more than any other person, but the past few weeks have been different."

Georgia thought back to the argument she had with Mr. Garrett and paled. "He was just being nice to me as the sister of Evangelina."

Ross shook her head. "Even Marcia Stuart noticed it."

She raised a brow. "Noticed what?"

"She noticed something," he said, lightly swirling his glass. "She thought for a moment you two were lovers. She said it was in the way you laughed."

"The way I laughed?"

Ross took a long sip of his drink. "In the way you *both* laughed."

Georgia colored. "What?" She almost laughed just then, trying to suppress her surprise. "Are you implying Mr. Garrett had feelings for *me*?"

Ross shrugged. "I am not implying anything. I am just pointing out an observation that was made."

Georgia shot another glance at Mr. Garrett and sighed. "No, you are wrong," she told him a little sullenly. "He only ever came to the house to see Evangelina."

Ross finished his glass. "Well, then I suppose we should wish them all the happiness," he grumbled.

Georgia nodded. "I suppose we should."

"You know," Ross said after a moment, "if push came to shove, you and I could always marry."

Georgia slowly turned her head to look at her friend. "If push came to shove?" she repeated incredulously. "What on earth do you mean by that?"

He shook his head. "That sounded worse aloud than it did in my head." He winced. "In my head, it sounded nicer."

"Please think a little harder before you say things like that," she told him. "Besides, do you really think I would want to marry a man who has been in love with my sister for the past four years?"

He took a deep breath and let it out slowly through his nose.

"I would always be wondering if you were wishing I was her instead," she explained. "Which would open the door to a new kind of misery for the both of us."

He cleared his throat with a nod. "I suppose you are right," he said staring into his empty glass. "I just thought it might save you from being shipped away. At least you would have a little more freedom."

Georgia heard the dejection in her friend's voice and reached out to squeeze his arm. "It was a lovely thought," she reassured him. "And

I do appreciate the sentiment, but it seems as if I am just doomed to a life of miserable loneliness, so I might as well make the best of it."

"Here, here!" he quietly exclaimed, raising his empty glass. "May we all venture into our miserable lives with the same amount of fortitude as you."

Georgia smirked at him.

"Good evening, Miss Hamilton."

Georgia turned to see Veronica Lewis smiling at her. "Miss Lewis," she said in reply.

"I have heard from your sister that you are to be a governess," Miss Lewis told her with a smirk. "Is it true?"

Georgia felt her stomach drop, but she forced a convincing smile onto her face. "Yes, it is true."

"How interesting," Miss Lewis breathed. "And where are you to go? Have you been hired yet?"

Georgia strained to keep the smile on her face. "No, not yet."

"You know, I have a cousin in Kent that might be interested," she informed her. "She has four children with a fifth on the way. Should I write to her?"

Georgia's lip twitched with annoyance, but she remained composed. "I do not see why not."

Miss Lewis's smirk broadened. "Perfect. I will do so tomorrow."

The two women gave half curtseys and Miss Lewis skittered to the other side of the room to spread her new intel, no doubt. If Georgia was not already the laughingstock of most of the women of Barchester, she would be now.

"Well, that was painful," Georgia muttered.

"I swear, she becomes more awful every time I see her," Ross said. "And it always surprises me. I always think, 'Well, she cannot get much worse than that,' and then she does!"

Georgia laughed. "I am glad I am not the only one to think so."

As the night progressed, Georgia wished more than ever that she was far away. She observed not only Mr. Garrett fawning over her sister, but William Henry trying to get her attention as well. It was painful to see her sister so much admired by a man she thought fancied her and by the man whose friendship she had missed.

Ross was kind and kept her company through most of the evening, but there were times when she was left alone. On one of those occasions, seeing that Mr. Garrett was relieved of Evangelina for a moment, she took it upon herself to talk to him. She strode across the floor with her shoulders back and head held high, trying to appear more confident than she actually felt.

"Mr. Garrett," she said in a small voice once he was within earshot.

He turned slowly to look at her. "Miss Hamilton," he replied, but not as warmly as he used to.

"I wanted to thank you for the beautiful journal you gave me," she told him. "It is so beautiful and perfect that I am not even sure if I could think of anything perfect enough to fill its pages."

"You are quite welcome," he said. "Though a simple note would have sufficed."

Georgia's heart sank. "I- I also wish to apologize for my awful behavior the last we spoke." She took in a deep breath. "You did not deserve such censure. I was angry at someone else, and you were an innocent scapegoat."

He didn't reply.

"I hope you can forgive me," she continued. "I do miss our conversations." She quickly curtsied, and hurried off before he could reply. Feeling like she needed a breath of fresh air, she stepped outside onto the veranda, but as she turned the corner she ran into William Henry.

Georgia gasped with surprise and took a step back. "I apologize," she quickly said and scurried away, but not before William grabbed her by the arm.

"Where are you running off to?" he asked, a sloppy smirk on his face.

"Let go of me, sir," she told him, trying to pull her arm out of his grip.

"What is the matter, Georgia?" he half slurred. "Do you no longer care for me? The last we met you seemed rather excited to see me."

"You are hurting me, Mr. Henry," she said a little louder. "Please let me go."

He released her, bowing slightly. "Forgive me," he said, still smirking. "I thought you might like to go for walk or something." He took a few steps toward her. "Perhaps you can finally have that kiss." He leaned in, puckering his lips when her hand planted across his face causing him to stumble and fall over a flowerpot.

Several of the guests outside laughed at the display.

"You struck me!" William exclaimed from the ground.

"You should know better than to take such liberties with me," Georgia retaliated. "I would never give you permission to touch me!" Embarrassed, Georgia nervously glanced around at the small number of guests that witnessed the occurrence and wondered how long it would take for them to spread what had happened. Her eyes watered, but she held firm as she made her way back inside, locking eyes with Mr. Garrett as she did so.

It was not long after the incident with William Henry that the whole party knew that Miss Georgia Hamilton struck him in the face. It was not long after that, that William Henry, in retaliation for his embarrassment, told those who would listen about his and Georgia's correspondence and how the whole time he thought he was talking to Evangelina. He proclaimed that Georgia hit him because she was still pining for him and was angry that he would not return her affections.

Laughter coursed through the room and several guests even snickered at her as they walked by.

"What is everyone going on about?" Ross asked her.

Georgia shook her head. "I have no idea," she replied.

Soon, the Hayes twins drifted over to them, whispering to

themselves before they stopped and smiled at Ross and Georgia.

"We have heard the most interesting story," Jennifer said.

Ross and Georgia exchanged glances.

"It is a rather juicy bit of gossip," Jessica confirmed.

"Sounds very intriguing," Ross replied, "but I can tell you we are not very interested in hearing it."

"Even if it involves you, Miss Georgia?" Jessica asked.

Jennifer giggled.

Georgia blanched. "What could be so interesting about me?"

The twins exchanged smiles.

"Mr. Henry has told us the most fascinating story," Jennifer told her.

"A story about a very big misunderstanding," Jessica added.

Georgia paled and she felt her knees become weak.

"He told us you are in love with him," Jennifer continued.

"And wrote your feelings to him, pretending to be Evangelina," Jessica concluded.

Georgia shook her head. "No," she said almost breathlessly. "That is not how it happened!"

The twins both giggled.

"Then how *did* it happen?" they said in unnecessary unison.

Georgia stood flustered for a moment, unable to speak as her embarrassment rose. Ross, in the meantime, became tense, balling up his fists in anger.

"That bloody coward is the one who—"

Georgia put her hand on Ross's arm stopping him from finishing what he was going to say. "Mr. Henry knows how it really happened," she told them. "If he chooses to lie because he is ashamed, then that is on him. I, for one, am not ashamed of how the true events took place. Nor do I care about his opinion."

The twins looked dissatisfied by this answer and moved away without another word.

"You are just going to let him spread lies about you?" Ross asked angrily.

"What does it matter?" Georgia told him. "That is the story they all wish to believe, so that is the story they will *choose* to believe. Whether or not I tell them the truth is irrelevant."

"Someone should teach William Henry a lesson in humility."

"I am sure one day that lesson will be learned. Whether or not he retains it is on him."

"Georgia, you do realize this will spread around town like the plague?"

She nodded. "Yes, I do," she replied, the sound of the twins' laughter ringing in her ears. She glanced up at the crowd, catching the eye of Mr. Garrett who was frowning at her. "It makes the thought of leaving this place actually tempting."

14

THE HUMILIATION GEORGIA EXPERIENCED AT THE PARTY FOLLOWED her home as Evangelina would not let her live it down. For days, her sister teased her relentlessly, triumphantly parading around her about it.

Evangelina incessantly goaded her, waving the incident in her face over and over, laughing at her torment without any regard for sisterly affection. She was even so bold and cruel as to laugh at her in front of their mother who did nothing more than to tell Evangelina to keep it down.

For the most part, Georgia ignored her. She would walk past her or leave the room without so much as a reply, but a week after the rumor of the false information, Georgia finally lost her temper.

"Are you so jealous of me, dear sister, that you are now pretending to be me?" she laughed. "Do you do it in the hopes that some unsuspecting man might fall in love with your words if they cannot fall in love with your face?"

Georgia took a moment to remove her glasses and place them on a table next to her book as her sister's words rang through her head. Years of her sister's verbal abuse mixed with the week of intentional cruelty finally came to a head, and, caring no more for societal expectations, Georgia lunged at Evangelina. She yelled in fury as she grabbed a handful of her sister's hair and pulled, slapping her in the face as she did so.

Evangelina, taken completely by surprise screamed like a banshee as she fell to the floor with Georgia on top. Georgia slapped her sister's face, strands of her sister's hair still caught between her fingers.

The two sisters both shrieked as they rolled and thrashed about on the ground, hands furiously grasping and smacking whatever they could. The ruckus was heard by most of the house including the staff. Most of them watched, unsure what to do, until the butler and Mr. Hamilton rushed over and finally pulled the girls, still kicking and screaming, apart.

"She has gone mad!" Evangelina cried as Georgia continued to reach for her.

"Let me go!" Georgia yelled still yearning to pull out more of her sister's bouncy hair, struggling against her father.

"That is enough!" their father bellowed causing them both to shrink in terror. "My office, the both of you, now!"

The butler who was holding Evangelina slowly let her go. "Do you wish me to escort them, sir?" he asked.

"No," Mr. Hamilton replied sternly. "If they know what is good for them, they will behave themselves. Is that not right, girls?"

The two sisters shot daggers at each other with their eyes but agreed to follow their father to his office in peace.

"Shut the door," Mr. Hamilton ordered as they entered.

Neither of the girls moved, not wanting to show weakness in front of the other.

"Evangelina, shut the door!" he yelled again.

Evangelina did as she was told before standing next to her sister, albeit several feet away, in front of their father's desk.

Georgia glanced at her trying to hide a smirk at her sister's mangled appearance. Her hair was a tangled mess, falling from its perfect array of bouncing curls and braids. A scratch ran across her cheek creating a welt and her lip was slightly swollen, a small trickle of blood falling from it. Though Georgia might not be proud of her actions, she was certainly proud of their outcome.

"What in the world has gotten into the both of you girls?" he interrogated. "I thought I had raised two sensible, or semi-sensible, young ladies. I did not know I was the father of two troglodytes instead."

For a moment, neither of the girls said anything.

"I am embarrassed and ashamed of your behavior," he continued.

"There can be no excuse for it, but, please, let me know what could be the reason for your childish actions."

"She is a wild animal, papa!" Evangelina cried. "She attacked me with no provocation! I was minding my own business when she jumped on me!"

Georgia huffed and refrained from rolling her eyes.

"She is not sane, papa!" Evangelina continued dramatically. "We must send her away as I am not safe around her! The sooner, the better! Who knows what she will do the next time she is near me!"

"That is enough, Evangelina," Mr. Hamilton said with a sigh, squeezing the bridge of his nose. "Georgia, what do you have to say?"

"I am sorry, papa," Georgia replied dejectedly. "I lost my temper. I was wrong."

Evangelina glanced over at her sister, confused as to why she wasn't telling their father the horrible things she said to her.

Mr. Hamilton sighed. "Evangelina, leave the room please," he said gently.

Evangelina looked between her father and her sister before turning silently, quickly exiting her father's office.

Georgia swallowed, a little nervous.

"What truly happened, Georgia?" her father asked her once they were alone.

She shook her head. "That is how it happened, papa," she replied. "I attacked Evangelina, and I am sorry for it."

Her father sighed. "I know how she antagonizes you," he confessed. "Was there nothing she said that made you attack her?"

Georgia met her father's eye. "Would it truly matter if she had?" she retorted. "*Her* words do not justify *my* actions."

Mr. Hamilton nodded. "That is very wise of you to say even if you did not follow your own advice."

Georgia gave a small smirk. "Learning from your mistakes is part of the learning process."

"And what of that young man at the Dorsets' gathering the other night?" her father ventured. "I heard you struck him as well."

Georgia pressed her lips together and blinked to keep the tears she feared would fall at bay. "I slapped him, yes," Georgia confessed. "But he deserved it. He was drunk and tried to kiss me."

Her father furrowed his brows. "He pressed himself upon you?"

"Yes, papa, and in his embarrassment, he began spreading lies about me," she told him.

"What kind of lies?"

Georgia shook her head. "Please, papa," she pleaded. "I do not wish to relive it. I want to let it go and move on with my life. The neighborhood will soon forget the rumors and pick up on something else. And when I am gone, it will not matter. They will soon cease to know I existed."

Mr. Hamilton took in a deep breath and sighed. He wanted to help his daughter, but respected her wish to drop the issue, so he did. "I have found you a family," he said after a moment.

Georgia's gaze fell to the floor.

"Or, I should say your uncle did," he corrected. "They are a family of two young girls and a boy living in London."

Georgia looked up.

"Your Uncle Richard says they are good friends. He speaks highly of them saying their last governess only left because she was getting married. He says they treated her like family. And they pay fairly, more than the typical twenty pounds a year."

She smiled weakly. "I suppose that is a positive."

Mr. Hamilton sighed again. "I am sorry, my dear," he whispered, his voice shaking. "I have failed you as a father."

Georgia frowned and shook her head. "Papa, no!" she protested, taking a few steps closer to his desk. "You have been a good and kind father to me. You have showed me love and respect and—"

"None of that matters," he told her, cutting her off. "None of that matters if I cannot afford to give you a comfortable life without sending you away." He shook his head. "You have been my greatest treasure all of these years. And I shall miss you."

Georgia's eyes welled up with tears. "When am I to leave?" she whispered.

"You are to leave from Louisa's house," he confirmed, clearing his throat.

"Am I still able to go, then?" she said, brightening up.

He nodded. "You leave for hers in a week. Then, you will be sent to the Wilmingtons' six weeks after that for your appointment."

Georgia walked around the desk and took her father's hand. "I will be alright, papa," she told him gently. "I will still be able to write my stories and read my books. That is all I really want. I will—" she cleared her throat and fortified her smile. "I will be fine. I promise."

He forced a smile for her. "I know, my dear. For you are the strongest of us all." He bent over and kissed her on the forehead.

15

Bittersweet was the day Georgia said goodbye to her family. She had packed what little had mattered to her in her suitcases and watched as a servant strapped them to the carriage. There was a sinking feeling in her chest as she stood there waiting for everything to be ready, a brief moment of anxiety that quickly dissipated.

She might not agree with the reasons she was being sent away, but she found herself wishing more and more not to be where she was. Perhaps this was the new start she needed. She took a deep breath and let it out slowly, accepting her fate.

Finally, when the servant informed her it was done, she turned and smiled at her father who was waiting outside with her. "It seems everything is ready to go," she told him a little awkwardly, unsure of what to say.

"Georgia," her father said softly, taking her hand. "I will not make you do this. If you change your mind and wish to come home, if you wish to cancel your employ with the Wilmingtons—"

"It is alright, papa," she sighed. "I am at peace with it." She smiled and kissed his hand. "I- I am almost looking forward to it."

"I have never admired anyone more than you, my dear."

She smiled weakly. "Tell mamma and Evangelina I will write very soon," she told him just as a means of delaying her departure. Her mother, who could not be bothered to watch her eldest daughter off, was still cross with her for having 'damaged' her sister's face though the scratch faded after a day. Evangelina had avoided her all together since their squabble.

Despite this, her father nodded. "I shall."

Georgia swallowed the pain of goodbye as her father planted a kiss on her forehead. "I shall make you proud, papa."

"You already do every day."

Georgia's father handed her into the carriage. She was just about to close the door when shouting could be heard from down the lane. Looking up, she saw Ross running his horse to meet her.

"I apologize," he said breathlessly as he made it to the carriage. "I accidently overslept." He got off of his horse, trying to catch his breath.

Georgia stepped back down from the carriage.

"It is nice of you to see my daughter off, Mr. Fairgrove," Mr. Hamilton said in greeting, an amused smile on his face.

Ross lifted a hand, still out of breath. "Sir." After recollecting himself, he stood straight and pulled a letter from his breast pocket. "Give this to my sister, would you?" he asked. "It would save me on postage."

Georgia huffed laughingly and snatched the letter from her friend. "Is this the only reason you rushed over here?"

He shook his head. "Why, were you expecting a parting gift?" he asked with a smirk.

She lifted a brow at him.

"Fine." He cleared his throat. "I might miss you and your scathing company."

Georgia laughed. "My scathing company?"

He nodded. "You have been rather cantankerous as of late."

"I think you have mistaken me for yourself," Georgia corrected with a smirk.

Ross thought for a moment. "I suppose you are right." He smiled. "But I shall miss you. You are one of the few level-headed sods around here."

Mr. Hamilton cleared his throat in mild disapproval.

She smiled at him. "Thank you for always being my friend." She reached out and squeezed his hand.

"You better write to me," he ordered as he helped her back into the carriage. "There will be no one here to make sure I am minding my manners if you do not."

Again, her father cleared his throat.

"If I can find the time, I promise I shall send you letters of the sternest instruction," she replied.

Ross bowed and stepped away from the carriage, standing next to her father.

Georgia smiled at them both for a moment before knocking on the side of the carriage informing the driver to pull away.

Georgia was surprised by being met at the halfway point sometime in the late afternoon by Louisa herself. The felicitousness of the occasion could not be captured in words as the two young women embraced each other, laughing joyously as they did so.

"Oh, Louisa!" Georgia exclaimed taking her friend's hands as she looked at her. "You are still glowing!"

Louisa, who had always been uncommonly pretty, smiled at her friend. "How could I not when I have not seen you in over a year? I am glowing with happiness!"

"I am so glad to see you," Georgia sighed, embracing her again. "There is so much to talk about that I could not begin to convey in any of my letters."

Louisa squeezed her friend's hands. "Come," she told her. "We have a several hours' ride ahead of us. We can begin there."

The three-hour drive to Louisa's was filled with laughter and a few tears. With restrained emotion, Georgia told her about her letters to and from William Henry and the horrible misunderstanding and embarrassment it led to. It was then to her friend's horror that Georgia relayed the state of her father's fortune and her forced appointment as a governess. In between all of that, she described to her the brawl between her and Evangelina.

"I cannot believe it!" Louisa gasped, holding back a laugh. "You and Evangelina coming to blows?"

Georgia shook her head. "I am ashamed of it," she sighed. "We were never particularly close, but in the past year in a half she has grown rather odious. Not just in her treatment of me, but of your brother. *They* used to be so close, but," she shook her head, "then, one day, it was as if she ceased to care for him."

Louisa cleared her throat and looked away for a moment. "Yes, I know," she replied softly. "Ross has been rather torn up about it."

"Yes, he has been more sullen than usual."

There was a brief silence between them.

"I am very sorry to hear about your father's misfortune, and, subsequently, yours as well," Louisa said reaching over and squeezing her friend's hand. "Your mother forcing you to become a governess. It is disgraceful and unmotherly."

Georgia's lips twitched into a smile. "I did not appreciate it at first, but I suppose I should be grateful. It allows me a way out of Barchester. I am not sure what other kind of life I would have expected If I am not to be a governess," she replied.

Her friend sighed heavily. "Georgia, men are a daft lot. They base what they want and what they think they need on sight alone without a care for who or what they are looking at. Their perception is too shallow to comprehend more than what their eyes perceive."

Georgia did not reply but she smiled at her friend with a nod.

"At any rate, I hope something awful befalls William Henry!"

"Louisa!"

"Well, I do," Louisa proclaimed matter-of-factly. "Awful man to do what he did. Curse him, I say. And I do not care who hears it!" She stuck her head out of the window. "Curse William Henry and all the men like him!"

Georgia laughed as she pulled her back in the carriage. "How embarrassing you are!"

Louisa smirked. "Well, as your friend there is a certain level of expectation of me."

Georgia raised a skeptical brow. "Which is?"

"To be on your side regardless of whether you are right or not- but we all know you are never wrong- and to humble you with spontaneous bouts of embarrassing situations."

Georgia laughed again, realizing in that moment just how much she had missed her friend the past year.

"Shall you have children soon, then?" Georgia asked after a moment's reflection.

Louisa narrowed her eyes playfully. "Might a husband and wife enjoy each other's company first before they add children to the equation?"

Georgia grinned. "Of course," she replied. "I was only thinking of myself. The sooner you have children, the sooner I can become *their* governess and begin my life of bitter servitude under your watchful eye. Old maid-ship might suit me after all, I think."

Louisa laughed. "Georgie, how terrible you are," she replied. "Must you always look on your life as so lonely? Governesses do marry, you know? It is not unheard of!"

"I should not be alone," she corrected. "If you were to have children, I would have them to keep me company. And as little chance as there is of my marrying and having any of my own, I must rely on you to have them for me."

Though Louisa knew her friend to be only half jesting, it hurt her. She hated how pessimistic she could be during times of melancholic reveries.

Georgia's melancholy soon melted away, however, as the carriage pulled along the drive up to the house. She gaped at her friend's manor in pleased astonishment. "Dear Louisa!" she exclaimed, seeing how perfectly situated the house was on a slight knoll, a lake stretching out in front of it.

"You are not disappointed at coming?" her friend teased.

"How could I?" Georgia replied. "I am only disappointed you have not invited me sooner." She sighed as she watched the swans swimming across the placid water of the lake, making the whole scene seem more majestic.

Louisa laughed. "Yes, it might seem like a bit much, but this is home."

They pulled up to the front and were helped out of the carriage by overdressed servants in wigs. They were then led inside where they removed their gloves and bonnets while Georgia continued to marvel at the inside of the house.

"Where is Mr. Barker?" Louisa asked a servant.

"He is in the parlor, ma'am," he replied. "Mr. Janes and Mr. Stokes are with him."

"Oh," Louisa said in slight surprise. "Thank you, Harry." She took her friend's arm under hers and led her down the marbled halls.

"Louisa, why did you not do a better job of describing this place to me?" Georgia gently scolded her friend.

"What, and sound like I was boasting?"

Georgia's eyes moved about the walls, trying to take in the paintings and tapestries that covered them. "There is no room for modesty now that I have seen the place. I wish you would have boasted away!"

They entered the parlor where the three men had been conversing, waiting patiently for their arrival. The two guests looked hopeful as the women stepped forward, but disappointment soon littered their faces when they realized Mrs. Barker's friend was not as pretty as either had wished, though neither of them were particularly handsome themselves. They both, however, bowed in greeting when introduced.

"Miss Hamilton," Louisa's husband Gregory Barker said, "allow me to introduce you to Mr. Stokes and Mr. Janes."

Georgia smiled pleasantly and curtseyed. "It is a pleasure to meet you both."

"We heard Mrs. Barker was receiving a guest today and thought we might band together to form a small welcoming party," Mr. Janes said, a man in his late thirties or early forties with dusty red hair streaked with gray that bounced about the top of his head. His smile animated his face as he rocked back and forth on his heels.

"We were also promised dinner," Mr. Stokes added seemingly bored, but managing to smile. He appeared younger than Mr. Janes physically, but Georgia could tell he lacked the older man's energy.

"Your welcome is much appreciated," Georgia told them both.

"Mr. Stokes is a lawyer here in Derbyshire," Louisa informed her, "and Mr. Janes is the vicar."

Mr. Stokes looked proud while Mr. Janes bowed modestly.

"You both must be rather tired," Mr. Barker surmised. "Why do you not freshen up? The dinner Mr. Stokes has been anxiously awaiting should be ready soon."

The anticipated dinner was soon announced and the party of five met again in the dining room with Georgia not so subtly placed between the two bachelors. Mr. Janes was pleasant enough, engaging her in conversation, pleased himself that Georgia needed little encouragement. Mr. Stokes, however, barely said little as he only seemed interested in his food.

"Do you walk at all, Miss Hamilton?" Mr. Janes asked her.

Georgia took a moment to swallow her food. "Yes, I often enjoy the peace a beautiful walk brings me," she replied.

"You are more for walks than riding?" Mr. Stokes inquired in a partially judgmental tone, barely looking up from his plate.

"Yes, I am not a great rider, I am afraid," Georgia informed them. "I suppose I am not comfortable entrusting my life to a creature with its own mind."

Mr. Stokes let out a small huff as he took another bite.

"I could not agree more," Mr. Janes said. "I would much prefer to put my own two feet to use. The exercise is good for the soul."

"I like that," Georgia agreed. "It *is* good for the soul."

"Do you play the piano at all, Miss Hamilton?" Mr. Stokes asked still not looking up from his dinner.

Georgia shot her friend a smirk who tried not to laugh. "Unfortunately, Mr. Stokes, though I have a great love for music, I am terrible at the piano," she confessed. "My mother often complained that only a true lady could play, but my poor little hands have never been good at reaching the keys."

Mr. Stokes sucked on his teeth for a moment. "That is a shame."

"Yes, it is," Georgia continued. "Especially since, even though I am terrible, I still try my hardest to play."

"Georgia is not one for giving up easily," Louisa said.

"That is a good quality to have," Mr. Janes stated with a nod.

Georgia smiled at him earnestly. "Thank you."

Mr. Stokes left not long after dinner, but Mr. Janes lingered well after, talking to Georgia about her opinions on ideologies and their influences on society.

"I think morally we view ideologies as good, often trying to carve out a path with them as the tools, but as humans, we often fall short," Georgia told him.

"For example?" Mr. Janes encouraged.

"Well, we are told we should not covet, that we should love thy neighbor," Georgia explained, "yet, we often love our neighbor to their face and then take every opportunity to judge them when they are not around."

"We?" Louisa inferred with a grin. "I hope you are not implicating anyone here."

Georgia smiled back. "I am not saying you in particular are guilty, but certainly we have all done it at one time or another. I believe most of us wish to do good, and we believe that we are, but we also fail to see our own shortcomings. It is only after someone points them out, and then after a short time coming to terms with them, are we able to better ourselves."

Mr. Janes smiled in admiration at Georgia. "Again, I agree with you. Everything you say is how I feel, yet, you say it much more eloquently. I wonder if I could ask your advice on a sermon or two of mine."

Georgia felt herself blush and her breath catch in her throat. "I am sure I would be glad to be at your service, though I do not know under what authority I should be giving you advice."

"Under God's authority," he replied firmly. "That is the only one that matters."

The vicar left soon after that conversation with a deep bow and a lingering look at Georgia.

"I think the vicar was impressed by you," Louisa told her a little too triumphantly.

Georgia looked at her friend with a raised brow. "I know what you are trying to do," she replied accusingly.

"Do?" Louisa repeated. "I am not trying to do anything."

Georgia sighed. "You knew Mr. Janes and Mr. Stokes would be here when we arrived, didn't you?"

Louisa avoided her gaze for a moment. "I might have."

"And what do you expect to happen?"

Louisa huffed at the accussation. "I do not *expect* anything to happen!" she proclaimed. "I just do not want to see my friend consigned to a life of self-imposed loneliness. You deserve so much more than that, Georgia!"

"Sometimes it is not about what one deserves," Georgia told her. "Sometimes you are just dealt a terrible hand and you make of it what you can." She shook her head. "I do not wish to have my hopes ripped apart again for one of your silly schemes. Please, do not force these men on me."

Louisa pursed her lips.

"Especially not Mr. Stokes," Georgia added. "He is rather," she paused to look for the right word, "emotionally vacant."

Louisa chuckled. "Alright," she finally agreed. "I will not force anyone on you while you are here, but I honestly do think the vicar thought kindly on you."

Georgia playfully narrowed her eyes at her friend. "Good night, Louisa," she said turning to leave the room.

Louisa smirked as she watched her friend walk away.

"I assume she does not know you only invited Stokes to make Janes look more appealing?" her husband said over his book.

"Shh!" Louisa shushed him. "You will ruin my plan."

16

WHATEVER PLAN LOUISA MIGHT HAVE LAID FOR HER FRIEND AND MR. Janes barely needed any encouragement. Mr. Janes, a man almost in his forties, had never married, not because he never had the desire, but because he thought most of the women he met with were not worthy enough to be the wife of a vicar.

Vanity often plagued the young minds of the women in his youth, and he grew to scorn their behavior, though respect them as children of God. That was not what he saw when he looked at Georgia. She was not pretty, to be sure-or at least not in the traditional sense- but she held herself with such confidence and spoke with such conviction that he could not help but find her intriguing.

Beauty was, after all, in the eyes of the beholder, and as a vicar, who was he to believe otherwise? Therefore, he made it a mission to visit the Barkers and Georgia almost every day he could.

Louisa herself was rather surprised that Mr. Janes took to her as quickly as he did. It was not that she didn't believe her friend capable, she just thought it would take more effort on her side to throw them together. The fact that it was falling into place so easily was almost disappointing.

Nothing made this more evident than when the Barkers brought Georgia to a public ball in town the week after her arrival. Mr. Stokes, already having told half the town of Georgia's mediocrity, met them with a stiff bow. He acknowledged Georgia saying what a pleasure it was to see her again, yet did not ask her to dance.

A few people eyed her with interest- a new face in an old crowd- as she walked among them, but it was Mr. Janes' reaction that caused a stir. Being the town vicar, he was known by almost everyone and they watched as he politely pushed through the crowd to meet Georgia with a low bow.

"My dear, Miss Hamilton," Mr. Janes said, "would you honor me with a dance?"

There were a few gasps from those in attendance close enough to hear and a whisper soon spread across the assembly.

"Of course, thank you, Mr. Janes," Georgia replied, not realizing the importance of the gesture.

Louisa, however, seemed a little surprised.

He stood and straightened his jacket, a smile lighting up his face. "I shall collect you when the dance starts then," he told her with a nod before making his way to the back of the assembly room.

"Was that a little bizarre?" Georgia whispered to her friend.

Louisa shook her head eagerly. "Not at all," she replied. "You know vicars; they mean well but are a bit of a strange lot."

Louisa took her friend around the room, introducing her to her neighbors and acquaintances, and Georgia watched as the eyes that had first met her with scrutiny and indifference, lit up with interest. Some of them even asked her questions.

"Are you the Godly type, then?" one older woman asked with a smile.

"Uh, yes, I do attend church regularly and try to behave as a good Christian should," Georgia replied.

"Our vicar is a good man, is he not?" another woman asked her.

"He is very kind," Georgia agreed.

"I do hope you are here to stay," one of the elder gentlemen told her.

"Oh, I do not think—"

"It is about time Mr. Janes settled down," he continued.

Georgia blinked at him for a moment until the very gentleman came to claim her for the dance. He bowed at his parishioners and apologized for taking Georgia away to which they all smiled and offered him encouragement.

Georgia was not expecting Mr. Janes to be a good dance partner but found herself pleasantly surprised by his gracefulness. Playful as she ever was, she told him so.

He smiled proudly. "I am glad to hear it," he replied. "I do not often dance."

"Is that so?" she asked. "Why should you not? Dancing is a harmless distraction, I believe, though I myself do not dance more than a few times when at a ball."

"I agree it is a harmless distraction," he began, "however, I often notice that dancing with someone or asking them to dance, often leads to misunderstandings or expectations."

Georgia frowned for a moment. "I suppose women with their heads in the clouds, or men who think too highly of themselves, might interpret a dance differently. A young woman might perceive a man asking her to dance as a sure step toward falling in love, while a man might perceive a woman's acceptance of his request as an assurance of her affections."

"Again, you have very eloquently described exactly how I feel on the subject!" Mr. Janes exclaimed. "You certainly have a way with words, Miss Hamilton."

Georgia laughed. "I am glad someone thinks so. My mother, however, might disagree with you. She might tell you I am too opinionated."

"Well, she is not here, is she?"

Georgia smiled with a sigh of relief. "No."

The dance soon ended, and Georgia parted ways with Mr. Janes satisfied with her new friend. However, she did not realize that her observations of how the simple act of dancing with someone could lead to more than one intends would pertain to the man with whom she had been dancing. Her acceptance of his offer to dance was seen as encouragement by not only him but by everyone else in attendance.

It became a little more apparent, however, as the night wore on and Mr. Janes asked her to dance another time. Again, everyone looked on, pleased with the scene and what it might mean for their vicar whom they all loved. After the second dance, more of the town's people seemed interested in her, asking her more questions- some borderline impertinent- about who she was and where she came from.

"Georgia likes to write," Louisa told a few of them. "Growing up we would always have writing competitions between her, my brother, her cousin, and myself, and she would almost always win!"

"Oh," said an old woman introduced as Lady Beverly skeptically. "And what would you write?"

"Just little poems or short stories mostly," Georgia replied.

"She is rather clever," Louisa boasted.

"Well, clever I suppose is good," Lady Beverly replied. "It shall keep him interested."

"I beg your pardon. *Him?*" Georgia repeated, confused.

"It was lovely seeing you again, Lady Beverly." Louisa pulled her friend to the other side of the room. "You must not pay her too much attention," she told Georgia when they were far enough away. "She is getting rather old and is prone to say whatever she is thinking no matter how ridiculous."

Other such statements were made throughout the evening—though not always in the presence of Georgia—about the townspeople's satisfaction or complaisance with the idea of Georgia as the vicar's wife.

"A vicar should settle down," one person said. "And, at his age, I do not think he could get anyone much prettier than her."

"A vicar's wife should be plain," said another. "It makes him humbler, and a humble vicar is more dutiful."

"What was wrong with that woman a few years ago?" asked a third. "She was more attractive than this one, but I guess the Lord knows what he is doing."

"She must have some good qualities, for she is not much to look at," was another comment.

Most of the whispers went unnoticed by Georgia and the vicar as they remained close in conversation most of the evening. At a certain hour, however, with it being a Saturday, Mr. Janes regrettably left in order to prepare for the following morning's sermon.

Georgia, unable to hold back her violent yawns any longer, wished to soon follow suit and said as much to her friend who had been waiting for an excuse to leave herself. Her husband, who always preferred a book to large gatherings, quickly ordered their carriage to be pulled around and they were soon off.

"I am quite pleased with the people of this town," Georgia said, covering her mouth as she yawned again. "They have all been a very strange, interesting, and inviting lot."

"That is because they believe you and Mr. Janes to be—"

"Good friends!" Louisa exclaimed, interrupting her husband.

Georgia gave her friend a skeptical look. "Mr. Janes does not make a habit of dancing, does he?"

Louisa feigned confusion. "What do you mean? I am sure I have seen Mr. Janes dance on several occasions."

"He told me himself that he does not make it a habit to dance," Georgia challenged her.

Louisa shook her head and waved a hand indifferently. "Oh, of course, he does not dance the whole night away, but he does dance. Does he not, dear?"

Mr. Barker looked taken aback at being pulled into their conversation and took a moment to clear his throat before agreeing with his wife. "Yes, he dances a reel or two at gatherings, I suppose."

Georgia sighed. "Well, I am on to you, Louisa. I know you are up to something."

"I do not know what you are talking about," Louisa replied innocently.

"I suppose we shall find out soon enough."

The sermon given by Mr. Janes the next day was given with more fervor than any of his others. He had always been a good orator and spoke eloquently, but the emotion that exuded from him for that particular Sunday made it difficult for even the usual nappers to not pay attention. He walked about the pulpit, using his arms to emphasize his points on morality and what it means in modern society.

His face was brightened by his smile, and, though he was not what one would call handsome, he had never looked more so. His energy did not fail him as he waited by the door to wish everyone in attendance a *blessed* day. A few of those parishioners lingered to see his reaction when Georgia walked out, and they were not disappointed.

Mr. Janes spoke with her for at least a full minute longer than anyone else, laughing heartily at something she had said. Satisfied, they dispersed, convinced that their vicar would soon be engaged.

17

Georgia sighed as she looked at her journal. She ran her fingers over the golden bird for the thousandth time before opening it and staring at its blank pages. She wanted to write in it. She wanted to fill its pages with something, but no matter how many times she dipped her quill into the ink well and hovered over the pages, nothing came to her. She was ready and willing to write, yet her mind would not allow her to push through the veil of her imagination. She closed the journal again after a minute, dissatisfied by her lack of inspiration.

There was a light rapping on her door and Louisa popped her head in. "I was wondering if you would like to take a walk."

Georgia smiled and stood. "That sounds wonderful," she replied.

"That is a pretty journal," Louisa said motioning with her head.

Georgia smiled and ran her fingers over it again. "Mr. Garrett gave it to me," she informed her.

"Adam Garrett? Of Cornwall?"

Georgia nodded. "Yes."

"That was very kind of him," Louisa commented a little cautiously. "But how are you acquainted with him?"

Georgia nodded again. "His aunt and uncle are the Dorsets."

"Ah."

"I told you how we met in Barchester while he was visiting his aunt and uncle, did I not?"

Louisa nodded slowly. "Yes, but I did not realize you were on gifting terms."

Georgia laughed. "Gifting terms?" she repeated. "I am not even sure what that means. He only gave it to me because I mentioned how there was nothing more inspiring than a blank sheet of paper to a writer. Though, I haven't felt very inspired as of late." She sighed with a smile. "Besides, he read *The Winds of Westbrook* and is hoping I could write another. So I am sure he thought this would help."

Louisa reached out and fingered the bird as Georgia had done. "And Mr. Garrett gave this to you? It seems rather," she paused for the right word, "special." She studied her friend to gauge her reaction.

Georgia smiled softly as she looked at the journal. "We had become quite good friends during his visit. I have never had pleasanter conversations with anyone, except for you. He would come to see Evangelina but was never disappointed to find only myself if she was out. He was very kind to me though I was terrible to him in the end," she confessed. "I said some very unwarranted things."

Louisa looked surprised. "*You* were mean to *him*?"

Georgia nodded guiltily.

"What on earth would possess you to be mean to a man as kind as Mr. Garrett?"

She sighed. "I am ashamed to say I was and am even more ashamed of *what* I said!

"Things you will tell me as we walk, I hope."

Georgia smiled a little abashedly. "Come, it is not a long story, but it does not put me in a very good light."

Louisa heard in astonishment the harsh words her friend had thrown at Mr. Garrett, shaking her head while she listened. "Dear, Georgia," Louisa said a little breathlessly, "I was not aware you had the ability to be so cruel!"

"It does not forgive what I said, but it was just after Mr. Henry had visited and realized he mistook me for Evangelina," she explained. "Poor Mr. Garrett just received the brunt of my anger."

Louisa raised a brow at her friend. "That is very unlike you."

"I know."

"That along with the incident with your sister, should I be concerned?"

Georgia sighed. "No, I do not think so. I believe I had just had enough. I have been putting up with being the object of Lina's jokes for so long, I threw my composure to the wind. It is with my behavior toward Mr. Garrett I am truly ashamed." She gave a small shrug. "At any rate, a little truth has never hurt anyone. Perhaps, I put him into perspective."

"Oh, Georgia, if that is what you believe, then you have gravely misjudged Mr. Garrett," Louisa told her.

Georgia looked at her friend inquiringly. "How do you mean?"

"For one, Mr. Garrett *has* had his fair share of disappointments," Louisa pointed out. "His mother, who was an angel, according to Gregory, died when Mr. Garrett was only nine. His father never quite got over her death and apparently drank himself into an early grave. He was an orphan before his sixteenth birthday."

"That is awful," Georgia commented, feeling her stomach twist into knots of embarrassment as she thought of what she had said to Mr. Garrett that day. "I had no idea."

"There is more," Louisa warned her. "One of his sisters, to whom he was closest, died in childbirth a year after that and the child expired with her."

Georgia gasped audibly. "Oh, Louisa, I am a monster to have said what I have said!"

"If you think that now, then I do not know what you will think when I am done," Louisa replied.

"There is more then?"

Louisa nodded almost imperceptibly. "About three years ago, Mr. Garrett met a young woman, very beautiful, charming and elegant," Louisa began. "He fell in love with her very easily and soon proposed."

Georgia listened with apprehension.

"However, it was overheard by some of his acquaintances of her bragging about how rich she was to become. She did not care for him at all, but only for his money."

"How awful!"

Louisa nodded. "Gregory heard her boasting about it himself and decided that he needed to inform Mr. Garrett." She shook her head.

"He had been devastated and at first could not believe it, but after more than one person confronted him about it, he knew it was true."

"Poor Mr. Garrett," Georgia whispered.

"It was not long after that it was discovered that she had been having an affair with a married man."

Georgia gasped. "Poor Mr. Garrett! To discover the woman he loved was not who she portrayed herself to be."

Louisa nodded. "Gregory says he has not been the same since."

Georgia let out a somber sigh. "I have done him a great injustice, Louisa."

Louisa raised a reproachful brow at her. "Yes, you have.

"Louisa, Evangelina does not love Mr. Garrett," she blurted out. "My mother is forcing the relationship because she is hoping it will save us from having to declare bankruptcy and having my father dragged to debtor's prison!"

"You are right," Louisa agreed. "Evangelina does not love Mr. Garrett."

Georgia frowned. "Why do you say it like that?"

Louisa sighed and shook her head. "I am sorry. I should not have said anything. Ross will be very cross with me."

"Ross?" Georgia repeated. "What does he have to do with anything?"

Louisa paused for a moment before shaking her head. "I am sorry, Georgia, but I cannot say anything. I have promised."

"There you are!" came the voice of Mr. Janes, catching up to them fast.

Georgia looked at Louisa. "Promise what?" she whispered.

"Never mind," Louisa replied, smiling and waving at Mr. Janes as he approached them. "Mr. Janes! We were not expecting you today!"

"Forgive me. My mother wished to get out of the house today, so I invited us to tea at your fine residence. I hope I am not terribly inconveniencing you."

Louisa smiled. "Not at all. It has been ages since I have had the pleasure of your mother's company outside of church."

Mrs. Janes was a woman of quick judgment with scrutinizing cat-like eyes. She was most likely a couple of decades older than her son, but her sharp tongue and sense of humor made her appear much younger.

She quickly sized Georgia up as soon as she walked into the room and before she sat down at the table. "You are Louisa's friend?" she asked directly.

"Yes, ma'am," Georgia replied with a curtsey. "We have known each other since birth."

"Do you have siblings?

"Yes, ma'am, a younger sister. She only turned nineteen a few months ago."

Mrs. Janes nodded. "Does she look like you?" she asked.

Georgia felt her cheeks burn for a moment, but she smiled through it. "No, ma'am, my sister is much prettier."

"Mother, let us not bombard poor Miss Hamilton with a thousand questions," Mr. Janes said softly.

"Why should I not ask questions?" his mother shot back. "How else am I to know someone if I do not ask them questions about themselves?"

Georgia smiled, greatly amused. "It is alright. Sometimes questions asked of you are good. It helps you become reacquainted with oneself again."

At this, Mrs. Janes smirked. "What an interesting thought," she replied. "Are you an opinionated person then?"

Georgia pursed her lips for a moment. "I certainly give my opinion more than my own mother would like."

Mrs. Janes chuckled. "She would prefer you to be silent? I was never of that opinion," she said. "Women have just as much right to a voice as a man does."

It was Georgia's turn to chuckle. "I like that. I think I shall use it, if you do not mind."

Mrs. Janes held out a hand as if to say 'go ahead'. "By all means. Then we shall be alike and get along just fine."

Georgia was satisfied by her new acquaintance and found her to be a witty spirit with whom she could relate. Despite this, there were times during their tea she found herself distracted with thoughts of Mr. Garrett. She realized now how undeserving she had been of his friendship and how short her apology had fallen the last they met.

When the tea was over and the guests were leaving, Mrs. Janes expressed her wish to see Georgia again. It was soon decided that the vicar and his mother would join them next week for dinner. Mr. Janes, of course, saw this as a great encouragement. His mother rarely showed this much enthusiasm over a new acquaintance.

18

GEORGIA REREAD THE LETTER FROM HER FATHER, TELLING HER HE missed her. She had now passed over two weeks with Louisa and her husband and though she almost could not care less about what her mother and sister were doing, she missed her father terribly. And, she would continue to miss him. Three and a half weeks was all she had left before her appointment as governess and she was growing more nervous by the day.

She quickly scribbled him a letter in reply about her time at Louisa's and how much she was enjoying herself. She failed to mention her apprehensions about her future and her pending position. She did not want to worry her father more than she knew he was.

Footsteps in the hall alerted her to someone approaching the parlor and she stood in anticipation, expecting Mr. Janes, a frequent visitor. She was surprised, however, when Mr. Garrett was instead shown in.

"Mr. Garrett!" she proclaimed feeling herself flush. She looked about the room for a few seconds rather embarrassed by their first tete-a-tete since her mistreatment of him.

He bowed a little shyly. "Miss Hamilton," he replied. "Forgive my intrusion on your solitude."

She shook her head. "Not at all. I am just surprised at your being here."

He smiled with a nod. "I am here to discuss business with Barker."

"Oh, well, I am afraid he is not here," she told him. "Mr. Barker went into town with Louisa to run a few errands."

"That is all right. Do you mind if I sit?" He pointed to a chair.

"No, not at all!" She moved toward the couches as well, taking a seat across from him.

"Were you in the process of writing?" he asked motioning to her letter on the writing desk.

She smiled. "To my father."

He nodded again but said nothing.

Georgia felt her heart fluttering inside her chest. She wanted to apologize again for her behavior that day but had not the courage. Instead, she sat readjusting her glasses and wringing her hands.

"Have you been using your journal?" Mr. Garrett finally asked in a quiet tone.

Georgia smiled sheepishly. "To be honest, no," she confessed. "I take it with me almost everywhere I go, yet, I have not found the perfect story to write in it. A journal like that deserves a good, lasting story, not a fleeting one."

He chuckled softly.

"Does that sound strange?"

He shook his head. "Not at all. It sounds reasonable. If you find your inspiration, I will be glad to have supplied you with your means to transcribe it."

Her smile widened, but shyness prevented her from saying any-thing else on the subject and she soon looked away.

"I must tell you, I am in anticipation for the next novel by Lady H."

She bit her lip as she smiled, looking down. "Your encouragement means a lot to me. Thank you.'"

"You should always be encouraged to do what you love." He looked as if he wanted to add to what he said but hesitated, shaking his head slightly instead.

"Oh! Can I offer you any refreshments?" she quickly asked after a long pause, remembering her manners. "I am sure you must be tired from traveling. Forgive me for not asking you sooner."

"No, thank you. I actually arrived last night," he informed her. "I was looking at a large piece of property Barker and I are thinking of buying to renovate."

"Really?" she replied with curiosity.

He nodded. "It is in the poorer part of town here. We hope to make it a better place to live. Affordable and decent for the under-privileged." He shook his head. "The ramshackle buildings provided for them now are barely fit for a dog much less women and children."

"That is very good of you," Georgia said with genuine feeling.

"It is something my mother used to always want to do," he replied, his cheeks reddening slightly.

Georgia felt her own cheeks burn at the mention of his mother.

"She had always wanted to buy property and build affordable, comfortable housing for the less fortunate. Somewhere to keep them out of the poorhouses," he continued. "This is me channeling her dream."

"Your mother sounds like a wonderful person," Georgia said avoiding his eye for a moment.

"She was."

Georgia took a deep breath and let it out slowly. "Mr. Garrett, I believe I owe you an apology." She paused a moment. "I was mon-strous to you that day. The things I said—"

He held up a hand stopping her. "There is no need. You have already apologized, and I have already forgiven you."

"I would hardly call what I said to you on our last meeting suffi-cient enough for an apology. You have always been so kind to me; more than most people, certainly more than my own sister." She shook her head and cleared her throat, regaining her thoughts. "What I am saying is, you did not deserve such awful treatment. You have been a friend to me, and I would like us to continue to be so."

A small smile spread across his lips, and he nodded. "I would much prefer your friendship to anything else."

Georgia smiled, her stomach fluttering.

"Might I ask you a question, however? Even if it might sound a little impertinent?"

She bit her lip but nodded.

"The last evening we saw each other, at my aunt's, I saw you slap Mr. Henry."

Georgia's face flushed and her throat became dry.

"Might I ask what that was about?"

"He was intoxicated and tried to take liberties with me," she replied in a small voice. "He thought because I had showed interest in him before, that he could treat me in such a way. I was just letting him know I was not going to stand for it."

Mr. Garrett colored and looked as if he wanted to jump from his seat. "Why had you not told me?" he asked, his voice riddled with emotion. "I would have had him thrown out. He had no right to treat you in that way!"

Georgia was a little stunned by his outburst and was unable to reply.

Mr. Garrett cleared his throat and straightened his jacket. "Forgive me. I cannot abide men trying to take liberties with young women. It angers me greatly. I will make sure he never sets foot in my aunt and uncle's house. He is not a man of honor, and I would not want him associated with any of my acquaintances."

Georgia shook her head still too confused to be fully composed. "No, I believe I had been fooled on that point."

"He is the fool. Not you," Mr. Garrett gently corrected her, his features softening.

She smiled. "Thank you."

"Is it true, then? Are you to be a governess?" Mr. Garrett asked her after a brief pause.

Georgia cleared her throat and folded her hands in her lap. "It is true. I leave from here to go to my appointment in a little over three weeks."

"Is that what you want to do?"

Georgia blinked down at her hands for a moment before she shook her head. "No, it is not," she confessed to him. "What I want to do is live in a small cottage with a library where the books are stacked so high, they are a hazard to all who pass by them. I want to take long walks in the mornings and write throughout the day by an obnoxiously roaring fire surrounded by no less than three dogs."

Mr. Garrett chuckled lightly. "And why can you not do that?"

Georgia smiled weakly. "And who would keep me, Mr. Garrett?" She sighed. "I have made an honest amount from *The Winds of Westbrook* so far, but—" She shook her head and cleared her throat. "I am doing this because my family asked me to. We are not doing well financially, Mr. Garrett. I know I can tell you this because I know you will not tell a soul, but it is true. Our fortune is all but lost."

Mr. Garrett looked concerned. "I am very sorry to hear that. Is your situation dire?"

Georgia shook her head. "I believe everything will right itself eventually, but it does not look good right now."

Mr. Garrett stared at her, his eyes full of feeling for her situation.

"I must also tell you something that might shock you," she began. "It might hurt you even."

Mr. Garrett blinked. "What is it?"

Georgia struggled for a moment trying to find the right way to put it. "I do not believe my sister to be in love with you. In fact, I believe her to be completely indifferent."

At this, Mr. Garrett looked startled, his face flushing. "Why are you telling me this?"

"Because I do not want you to fall for her or be in love with her only to find out that she is only marrying you for your money. It is not right. You deserve better than that."

"You are telling me this out of concern because you believe me to be in love with your sister?"

Georgia nodded. "And I wanted to put you on your guard about her. I am ashamed to say anything against my family, but the misfortune we have come across has made us a little desperate. Please accept my apologies on their behalf."

Mr. Garrett looked as if he didn't know how to feel. "Thank you," he replied slowly. "I shall take what you have said into consideration."

"Are you staying here long?" Georgia asked after another lull in their conversation.

"I believe I shall be here for a week or two," Mr. Garrett answered. "There are a few things to work out with the property, but I would not mind staying for the company either."

"Yes, the people here are rather nice."

He smiled. "They are accommodating, yes." He fiddled with his hat. "I have always enjoyed coming here."

There was another pause between them.

"Would you not take tea," Mr. Garrett?" Georgia pressed. "I was just about to order some myself, after I finished my letter."

He finally nodded. "Yes, please."

She rang the bell for tea, satisfying her nerves.

"I hope what I had said earlier did not offend or hurt you, Mr. Garrett," Georgia told him. "I did not mean to do so."

He looked at her a little bewildered. "What do you think could have offended me?"

"When I informed you that my sister does not love you," she clarified. "I know it might have seemed rather harsh. But I do believe you deserve better than a woman who is only marrying you for your money."

"Why should I take offense?" he asked. "I should be thanking you for looking out for me as anyone who truly cared for me would do."

Her cheeks flushed a little at this. "Yes, I know, but if you love her, hearing something like that must be unbearable!"

"Miss Hamilton, I do not—"

"Adam Garrett, you fiend!" exclaimed a smiling Mr. Barker as he walked into the parlor.

Mr. Garrett stood and grasped his friend's hand. "Gregory Barker! You scoundrel!"

They both laughed.

"I see Miss Hamilton has been keeping you company," Mr. Barker stated.

Mr. Garrett nodded with a small bow to Georgia. "As always."

"Has tea been ordered, then?" Mr. Barker asked.

"Only a few minutes ago," Georgia told him.

"Ah, well, then that is enough time to talk a few minutes' business! Come, Garrett," Mr. Barker said patting his friend on the back.

Mr. Garrett shot Georgia a smile as he followed his friend out of the room.

"Mr. Garrett is here a few days earlier than expected," Louisa said entering the parlor. "Though I would never complain. He is rather nice to look at."

"Louisa!" Georgia laughingly scolded.

"Oh, do not tell me you do not think so!" Louisa shot back. "If you did, I would certainly call you a liar." She huffed loudly and fanned herself with her hand. "I think it is getting hotter by the day."

"It *is* still summer," Georgia reminded her.

"Well, I am done with it." Louisa sat down on the other side of the couch. "What did you and Mr. Garrett talk about?"

Georgia shook her head. "Nothing really. He told me of his plans of building housing in town for the less fortunate."

"Yes, he is truly a giving man," Louisa pointed out. "He is not even thinking of making money on the venture. It is almost pure charity."

Georgia smiled to herself.

"What is that?" Louisa asked causing Georgia to look up sharply.

"What is what?"

"That look you have on your face?" Louisa eyed her skeptically.

Georgia furrowed her brows. "I was not aware I had a look on my face."

"It was a look of contentment."

"Can one not look content without suspicion?" Georgia inquired.

"Most people, yes," Louisa replied with a smirk. "But it is not a look I often see on your face, Miss Georgia Hamilton. What are you thinking?" Her friend narrowed her eyes at her, sizing her up.

Georgia laughed and readjusted her glasses. "I am not thinking anything!" she proclaimed.

But that was a lie. She *was* thinking how handsome Mr. Garrett was and how content she felt knowing he had forgiven her.

19

Another week had gone by, and Georgia was less than three weeks away from her assignment and only a week away from her birthday. Both of which she was dreading. It had been a small consolation to have Mr. Garrett around though he had been so busy he was only able to make two dinners and a single tea since he had arrived.

One of those dinners was the same one that Mr. Janes and his mother came for. The two men had greeted each other with pleasant familiarity but parted with a hint of tension between them. It began with an innocent comment from Mrs. Janes, who, observing that Mr. Garrett was still unmarried, asked if he had any plans to do so.

Mr. Garrett blushed slightly and cleared his throat. "Yes, ma'am," he replied civilly despite the invasiveness of the question. "I do have *plans* but as I have often found out, plans do not always come into fruition. Even the simplest of plans could go awry."

Mrs. Janes seemed to have nodded in agreement. "Yes, I am sure my son could attest to that," she replied. "He had plans to marry a girl a few years back, but it was not meant to be. However, things tend to work out for the best. I believe his second choice suits him much more."

At this, Mr. Garrett looked over at Mr. Janes and Georgia further down the table conversing and smiling. He could see the look on Mr. Janes' face and recognized it for what it was. Infatuation.

He colored a moment, but soon recollected himself. "Is that so?"

The older woman nodded. "Miss Hamilton would make a good vicar's wife, I believe. She is not very pretty but has good moral values and a clever mind."

Mr. Garrett gave a strained smile. "Yes, she does," he agreed a little quietly.

"I am justly happy for them both," she stated.

"You talk as if it is a settled thing," he replied trying to laugh.

"Well," Mrs. Janes began with a shrug, "why shouldn't it be? They seem to enjoy each other's company and if both parties are willing, there is no reason for it not to be settled and settled as soon as can be."

After that Mr. Garrett barely spoke a word; he merely observed, taking in the scene around him. He watched Georgia's interactions with Mr. Janes trying to decipher if there were any true feelings behind her eyes for him.

A few times, he caught her eye causing her to smile softly in his direction. It was this that emboldened him. It was true, she was not the most handsome woman he had ever seen, but there was an intensity about her expression and a passion when she spoke that intrigued him, that continued to intrigue him since they first met. Finally, he walked forward and cleared his throat.

"Miss Hamilton," he said a little louder than he intended, drawing the whole room's attention, "I was wondering if you would join me for a phaeton ride around town tomorrow?"

For a moment, confused by such a strange action, everyone, including Georgia, blinked at Mr. Garrett. Mr. Janes eyed him suspiciously; Louisa did so with interest.

Mr. Garrett suddenly felt a little silly. "Do you remember the scheme I once proposed when I first arrived in Barchester? Perhaps we can finally have that ride."

Georgia could feel the heat rise in her cheeks and a flutter in her stomach. "Yes, I remember and would certainly be pleased to join you, but I have already promised Mrs. Janes to help her cut and hang herbs for drying."

"Oh," Mr. Garrett breathed.

"Perhaps, the following day, Wednesday," Georgia suggested.

Mr. Garrett nodded, thoughtfully. "Yes, I believe Wednesday should do just fine."

Wednesday would be fine as Mr. Janes intended to be out of town.

He had made it a point and set off the next day to Barchester so that he could ask Georgia's father for her hand in marriage with Georgia none the wiser. He intended to wait a little longer as he did not like the idea of rushing into something as important as marriage, but he feared that if he waited too long, she might be unobtainable.

No, he was not worried of her being attached to anyone else. She was too moral to lure a man in on false hope, especially if she had another one waiting in the wings. Besides, she wasn't pretty enough for that. She had been welcoming and warm, and most often encouraging to him. The fact that he had his mother's approval made the affair all the merrier.

But, soon, she would be gone. Off teaching other people's children who could not be bothered to spare the time to teach them themselves. Though, he believed she would make the best of teachers, and every child could benefit from a mind like hers, he felt securing her hand now was the best course of action as she was still young, and he was getting older. So, therefore, he went.

While Mr. Janes traveled to secure her father's permission, Georgia enjoyed her early afternoon with his mother sharing anecdotes as they clipped back herbs and strung them on the walls to dry.

"Are you enjoying your time here, my dear?" Mrs. Janes asked her when they were done.

"Yes, ma'am," Georgia replied with a hint of melancholy. "I am rather dreading going and I feel as if time has been going by so quickly." She sighed. "I shall be a governess before I know it."

"For as young as you are, I believe you to be rather wise," Mrs. Janes told her. "I think you would make a wonderful governess."

Georgia smiled. "Thank you."

Mrs. Janes patted her hand. "I see hesitancy in you," the older woman pointed out. "Fear not. Though this may be the plan for now, it might not be the one that lasts."

Georgia frowned slightly, not sure of her meaning; she left there, however, with a sense of hope. Maybe being a governess would be temporary, though she could not yet see a way out.

The following day, as promised, Mr. Garrett came to take Georgia for a ride around town. The early September weather was still warm, but the breeze had a promise of fall as they rode along.

"I understand your birthday is in a few days," Mr. Garrett stated.

Georgia nodded, pressing her bonnet to her head as the breeze picked up. "Yes, Friday," she replied with a sigh.

"You will be three and twenty?"

She nodded again. "Yes."

"We shall drive to the bookshop, then," he told her. "I will buy you whatever book you want."

She smiled. "I do not need presents, Mr. Garret, though the thought is very appreciated," she replied. "I merely want to pass my twenty-third birthday as quietly as possible."

"You will not celebrate?" he inquired incredulously. "Why should you not? You deserve some sort of celebration; everyone does."

Georgia chuckled lightly. "I gave up believing I deserve anything not too long ago, Mr. Garrett," she informed him. "I am a person just like anyone else. No better, no worse. Therefore, I deserve nothing better or worse."

"That is the first ridiculous thing I have heard you say," he declared.

Georgia laughed. "It is true!"

"Well, whatever you might believe, I believe you deserve at least something," he decided. "And if you will not pick out a book for yourself, I shall have to choose for you."

She laughed again. "I suppose you can do as you please," she conceded. "I cannot stop you as you are your own man."

He took a moment to look at her, slowing the phaeton as he did so. "Sometimes, I am not so sure I am," he told her cryptically.

She frowned. "How do you mean?"

He shook his head after a moment and focused his attention back on the road. "Forgive me," he replied. "It is a strange thing to say."

She placed a gentle hand on his arm. "It is alright," she assured him. "You do not have to tell me if you do not want to."

He glanced down at her hand for a moment before looking back up. "I am a reserved man, Miss Hamilton," he responded. "Emotions and feelings do not come easily to me, but when they do, I believe I feel them keenly and deeply."

Georgia regarded him for a moment, her chest tight, unsure as to where this conversation was going to lead.

Mr. Garrett shook his head after a moment. "There is something I feel- something I believe I must tell you."

Georgia felt her heart drop and her breath almost left her lungs.

"I believe I am in love," Mr. Garrett finally confessed. "There can be no other way to say what I am feeling- *how* I am feeling- except for that. I have not slept in weeks, and I am restless when I do! I barely eat; I find myself often distracted by my wishes. I am always thinking of what this person is doing and to whom she is talking; whether she is enjoying herself at this moment or if she is as miserable as I am."

Georgia bit her lip to keep it from trembling.

"I have a burning desire to know more about her; to hear her opinions on certain subjects; to hear her laugh at the ridiculousness of mine." He glanced at her a moment. "I am in a world of constant confusion because I am told I should not love this person, that I should be in love with someone else."

Georgia felt her eyes fill with tears and she looked away to hide them. "Mr. Garrett, please!" she said stopping him from going on any further. "Your words are making me uneasy. Perhaps, this is not something you should share with me."

He blinked over at her. "If I do not share them with you, then whom do you expect me to share them with?"

Georgia did not get a chance to answer when a stray dog ran into the middle of the road, growling and nipping at the horse causing it to rear up in fright before going into a full gallop. The carriage swayed dangerously as it went over the gravel path, making Georgia scream in trepidation.

"Hold on, Miss Hamilton!" Mr. Garrett roared over the sound of the wind rushing in their ears.

His hands gripped the reins tightly, causing his knuckles to become white as he pulled back with all his might, but the horse could not be persuaded to stop. It dashed half on the road, half off, kicking up dust and rocks as it went, and running a few other carriages off the road.

Finally, after a mile of chaos, the horse began to slow, but not before one of the phaeton's wheels struck a rock, breaking. Georgia let out a scream as the carriage teetered on the side of the road throwing her to the ground. Before she knew what was happening, there was a sharp pain in her head, and the world went black.

20

Georgia woke with a groan, squinting as she slowly opened her eyes. She pressed a hand to her head to stop it from throbbing, but it was no use, so she closed her eyes again and fell back on the pillow.

"You're awake!" Louisa exclaimed, rushing to her bedside.

"What happened?" Georgia asked groggily.

"You fell from the carriage after one of the wheels broke," Louisa explained. "The doctor says you shall be fine, however. You luckily only sustained a few scrapes and bruises."

"It feels much worse than that," Georgia mumbled. "I feel as if my whole body is broken." She groaned as she tried to sit up, Louisa helping her.

"Oh, do not be so dramatic," her friend teased. "Your glasses luckily fared better than you." She pulled the spectacles from the bedside table and handed them to her. "Not a scratch on them."

She took her glasses tentatively, placing them gently on her face. "How long have I been out?" she asked as she readjusted them.

"Only a couple of hours."

"What about Mr. Garrett? Is he alright?"

She nodded. "Yes, he has a few scrapes, but was not badly hurt."

Georgia exhaled loudly, relaxing into the bed. "I am glad," she said softly. "Where is he?"

"Pacing the garden," Louisa told her. "He was rather upset about the whole thing. He blames himself."

Georgia tried shaking her head, but a flash of pain coursed through her. She pressed the palm of her hand to her temple. "It was not his fault. That dog came out and scared the horse. Certainly, he cannot take credit for that."

Lousia didn't reply, she merely watched her friend for a few moments. "Georgia," she finally began, "what is the nature of yours and Mr. Garrett's relationship?"

"Relationship? What could you mean, Louisa? We are only friends," Georgia replied quietly, her stomach twisted in knots.

There was another pause.

"You do not think him to have feelings for you?"

"No," Georgia quickly replied, almost laughing, though the pain of the answer was more than just physical. "Do not be ridiculous. No, he is in love with someone else. He told me so today."

"Oh," Louisa said disappointedly.

"You said he was unhurt?" Georgia clarified.

"Yes, shall I go get him? I know he would wish to see you. He looked miserable when he brought you here."

"Please do not," she told her with a little more force than she intended. "I think I am going to rest a little longer. Tell him I am well and do not believe him to be at fault, but that I must rest."

Louisa smiled at her friend. "I shall take care of it for you."

GEORGIA SLEPT THE REST OF THE DAY WAKING THE NEXT MORNING feeling better. She slowly got herself dressed and made her way down the stairs where she was greeted by Mr. Barker. He bowed and congratulated her.

"You gave us a bit of a scare," he told her.

"Forgive me," Georgia replied. "And thank you for taking charge of my care."

He smiled at her, holding out his arm. "Come, let us breakfast."

Georgia took his arm and allowed him to lead her to the breakfast parlor where food was waiting for them. It was not until the smell of fresh bread and melted butter hit her nose, did she realize how hungry she was. She slowly ate, however, her head still light from her fall.

When she was done, she excused herself, wishing to take in the fresh air of the morning. She did not make it far when she became lightheaded and made her way to a bench in Louisa's garden. She sat for a few minutes alone, watching the birds flit about, when a shadow appeared behind her.

She turned to see Mr. Janes dressed in some of his best clothing, looking nervous. "Mr. Janes," she said pleasantly, "good morning. I had not realized you returned from your business trip."

"Miss Hamilton," he replied stepping forward, "I heard you had a fall."

She smiled with a nod. "Yes, but I am much better now. I feel rather bruised, but I thank God nothing is broken."

"Yes, thank God indeed," Mr. Janes agreed. "When my mother told me yesterday upon my return, I was rather concerned. I had half the mind to run here to check on you, but my mother advised against it. She had a letter from Mrs. Barker that you were resting. Mother said I should not disturb you."

"I am grateful for your concern," Georgia replied, "but your mother was right. I would have made poor company."

There was a strange silence between them. Georgia sensed that something was different, and, despite the heat, a chill ran across her spine, causing an involuntary shiver.

"Are you cold?" Mr. Janes asked. "Perhaps you should return."

Georgia smiled and gently shook her head. "I assure you, I am well."

He nodded. "I am glad." He cleared his throat. "I feared you would still be in bed. I went to the house to find you when I first arrived, but Mrs. Barker informed me you went for a walk."

"Yes, I was in want of a walk after breakfast. I thought the fresh air would do me good," Georgia explained. "I was overcome by light-headedness, however. Perhaps, I wished myself well more than I actually am."

He flashed a small smile and nodded. "There is no shame in resting."

There was another awkward silence for a few moments.

"Would you like to sit for a moment, Mr. Janes?" Georgia finally asked. "You seem rather pale yourself. I hope *you* are not unwell."

He cleared his throat and shook his head. "I am extremely well, thank you," he answered though shakily, avoiding her eye for a moment.

Georgia regarded him, unsure of his strange actions.

Mr. Janes cleared his throat again before taking a deep breath and letting it out slowly. "Miss Hamilton," he swallowed nervously, removing his hat and twisting its brim in his hands, "I am sure this will come as no surprise to you, for I believe I have made my intentions rather clear, but I have a great wish to make you my wife."

Georgia blanched and felt her skin prickle. She sat unmoving, too shocked to reply.

"The first night we met, I saw within you the image of my future companion," Mr. Janes continued. "Your sense of morality, wit, and all-around goodness, has helped me see that God has chosen you as my wife."

Georgia felt her eyes bulge and she looked away to hide her embarrassment.

"I know I will never be able to provide for you the way you must have grown accustomed to in your upbringing, but I shall strive every day in any way possible to show you how you are loved and adored, not only by God, but myself."

Georgia tried to breathe, but could not, her head spinning as she tried to make sense of what just happened.

Mr. Janes shifted uncomfortably where he stood before kneeling awkwardly. "I shall cherish you, Miss Hamilton, as a most beloved wife if you would do me the honor." He reached out and tenderly took her hand in his, bringing it to his lips.

Georgia was at a loss of words and merely stared as his lips grazed her knuckles before her hand was returned to her. She stuttered for a moment, looking almost everywhere except at Mr. Janes. Finally, after what seemed like an eternity, Georgia found her voice.

"Mr. Janes, I am beyond flattered and grateful at your mode of declaration. I could not—would not—ever expect such a proposal from anyone," she began almost breathlessly, stalling for time as she figured out what she wanted to say. "I am even more surprised that after such a short acquaintance you have found it within you to love me." She shook her head slightly. "This being said, I must beg you to allow me a day or two to think over your offer as a decision as lasting and binding as marriage should never be made in haste yet should be made with a clear mind."

Mr. Janes stood and kissed her hand again. "I do not oppose such a decision," he told her, a hopeful smile on his face. "It is a testament to your wisdom. I should also mention that I have met with your father and made the appropriate request for your hand." He pulled a letter from his pocket and handed it to her. "This letter was written by your father, entrusted to me for its delivery."

Georgia took the letter barely seeing it.

"I shall anxiously, and as patiently as I can, await your answer, Miss Hamilton." Mr. Janes bowed before putting his hat back on his head and walking the way he came.

Georgia sat alone, replaying the scene in her head over and over. Did that truly just transpire? Did she truly just receive an offer of marriage? Was this her way out? She pressed a hand to her mouth as she thought. Did Mr. Janes truly love her as he said he did? Was it possible she could inspire such feeling in someone?

She had been fooled once by pretty words, but Mr. Janes was so unlike William Henry. He was sincere and modest; he had chosen her having seen her first, and she respected him for it. But could she resign herself to a life with him?

After she was done forming the questions for which she had no answer, she remembered the letter in her hand. She looked down at it, recognizing her name written in her father's hand. She opened it slowly, unsure of what to expect.

My dearest girl, it began.

What happy news I have received today! I have met with Mr. Janes who traveled all the way here to ask me for your hand in marriage. You could not believe my surprise upon this proposal, not because I do not think you capable of securing a man, my dear, but because I would not have expected it after only having been at Louisa's for three weeks.

Do not take my surprise as a refusal, however. If this is the path and the man you have chosen, then I am more than elated. If you wed soon, I shall hurriedly write an apology letter to the Wilmingtons and explain why you must quit your appointment. Though, I must caution you from a speedy marriage to a man whom you barely know. A long engagement will be better so that you both may become more accustomed to each other's whims and fancies.

I am ecstatic my dear. Mr. Janes seems like a very good man, and I have heartily given him my consent. I have always wished happiness for you, Georgia. You are the most deserving of it.

With all my love, your affectionate father.

Georgia did not realize she was crying until the first tear fell onto the letter, spattering and causing the ink to run. Upon hearing approaching footsteps, she quickly wiped her eyes dry and blotted the tears from the paper before folding it back up.

"Mr. Janes did not stay long," Louisa said as she sat down next to Georgia.

"No," Georgia agreed. "He came to check on me."

Louisa blinked at her friend. "It is alright, Georgia," she told her. "I know what he came to do."

Georgia looked over at her.

"Men do not dress in their best clothing merely to 'check' on someone," Louisa explained.

Georgia laughed softly through her nose, but made no reply.

"So?" Louisa said after a long silence.

"So what?"

Louisa scoffed. "What did you say in response?"

"I have not given him an answer," Georgia told her. "I asked him to let me think about it for a day or two and he agreed."

Louisa patted her friend's hand. "There is nothing wrong with that. I think it is a wise decision."

"No, you do not," Georgia corrected her. "I can hear the strain in your voice."

Louisa sighed with a smile. "Must you know me so well?" She looked at her friend a little sternly. "Fine, I do not understand what there is to think about! You obviously like Mr. Janes, do you not?"

"Like him, yes, he is a good man with whom I can easily converse with, but I do not *love* him," Georgia answered a little heatedly. "And I do not see how he could love me either."

"You do not give yourself enough credit."

"It is not because I think myself unable to 'capture' a man as people say; it is because of the short duration of our acquaintance," she explained. "But now I see that almost everyone has decided that we should be together." She shook her head. "I do not want what other people believe or think to sway my decision. I want to make it on my own."

Louisa nodded. "That I can understand."

Georgia smiled. "Thank you."

"Though he did travel all the way to see your father just to ask him for your hand in marriage!" Louisa exclaimed. "If that is not a gesture of love and dedication, I do not know what is."

"How did you know he went all the way to Barchester to meet with my father?"

Louisa shrugged, stuttering slightly. "A, uh, little birdy might have told me."

"You mean Mrs. Janes?" Georgia lifted a brow.

"Oh! She would not make a horrible mother-in-law. She thinks fondly of you, too!"

Georgia thought for a moment before shaking her head. "Would you have married Mr. Barker if you did not love him?"

Louisa paused and looked down at her hands. "No," she confessed after a moment or two. "I would not have resigned myself to a loveless marriage."

Georgia nodded. "I know I am unlikely to receive any more proposals in my lifetime, but that does not mean I have to settle."

"But who is to say you will not fall in love with him once you are married?" Louisa suggested with a shrug. "There is room in a marriage to get to know one another."

Georgia looked down at her hands, her father's letter still neatly folded in them. She took a deep breath and let it out slowly. "I shall give him my answer tomorrow," she concluded.

"On your birthday?"

Georgia nodded. "Yes, but until then, we shall not discuss it. I want no words of persuasion either way. The decision, as I have said, shall be mine and mine alone."

Louisa nodded. "Understood." She shifted uncomfortably unable to keep herself from asking what she wanted to know. "Other than your lack of love for him, is there another reason you hesitate?"

Georgia glanced quickly at her. "Another reason?" she questioned. "What other reason could there be?"

Louisa sighed as she looked at her friend. "Do you hesitate because your heart already belongs to another?"

Georgia paled before blushing.

"There would be no shame in it if you were, Georgie," Louisa gently goaded. "No one could ever blame you for such a reason as this."

She averted her gaze to the grass and watched for a moment as a warm summer breeze fluttered through it. "What would that matter?" she finally replied just above a whisper. "If I were in love with another, it would signify if those feelings were not returned. I would be in the same position I am now, would I not?" She forced a small smile.

Louisa wanted to tell her that she had not answered her question, but the look in Georgia's eyes begged for silence on the subject. Instead, she got up from the bench and held out her hand to her. "Come, let us go inside. I have a need to hear you play horribly on the piano."

Georgia laughed as she took her friend's hand. "I do not know what it is about you and your brother wishing so cruelly to make me play."

Louisa smirked. "If you cannot tease your friends, are you even friends at all?"

Georgia laughed again despite the overwhelming decision looming over her.

21

Georgia awoke on her birthday with feelings of trepidation. The day was supposed to be a celebration of her, yet, it represented a change greater than her gaining another year. Today she would decide whether she was going to resign herself and the rest of her life to governess-hood, or to the life as a vicar's wife.

The apprehensions of the day plagued her so much the night before that she rose feeling unrested as if she barely got any sleep at all. Despite these feelings, she put on a happy face, as was expected, and drifted downstairs to a barrage of congratulations from Louisa and her husband.

She thanked them politely, going through the emotions of the day as normal, trying to put off her decision until she could be alone. There was not much time to think since Mr. Janes, his mother, Mr. Garrett, and a few others were expected at dinner. The thought of making such an announcement with so many people gouged at her insides, but she was determined that she would.

She was a woman after all; it was time to grow up.

To her chagrin and, yet, satisfaction, Mr. Janes arrived before anyone else. Louisa flushed for her friend, offering her a smile of encouragement when he was shown into the parlor just as they had sat for tea.

"Mr. Janes," Georgia blushed in uncontrollable embarrassment, "you are here very early."

"Forgive me," he replied with a deep bow. "I wanted to be one of the first to offer my congratulations on your birthday."

Georgia smiled but could not meet his eye. "Thank you," she answered shyly. "Will you not take tea with us?"

Of course, he did. He readily sat down talking more feverishly than before on subjects Georgia did not have the state of mind to comment on further than a few words. Regardless, she listened intently, trying to grasp whether her feelings for Mr. Janes were that of a mere friend or whether they could grow into something more.

She blushed deeper as she thought of this, hoping she could come up with an answer soon, to have it over and done with before the rest of the guests arrived.

"Are you well, Miss Hamilton?" Mr. Janes asked her. "You seem quite flushed."

Georgia took a deep breath and smiled. "Yes, I believe I am just a little warm," she told him, putting her tea down.

"Would you fancy a walk?" Mr. Janes inquired slowly.

Georgia quickly shot her friend a look, but Louisa wisely turned her head to avoid it. "Yes, a walk would be lovely," she finally replied after a brief hesitation.

Mr. Janes stood and offered his hand which Georgia took tentatively, allowing him to help her from her seat. He gently placed her hand on his arm and escorted her outside where the air was just beginning to feel like autumn. Georgia sighed in satisfaction.

They walked for a time in silence, mentioning only the weather or commenting on the occasional bird. When they had walked for about a quarter of an hour in silence, Mr. Janes stopped and turned to Georgia.

"Forgive me," he said, looking at her with hope-filled eyes, "I know I said I would give you time, but I am in utter agony. I could not sleep last night as your answer was all I could think about." He cleared his throat. "I know I am not the most handsome of men, nor am I the richest, but as I told you before, I will spend my days making up for what I lack in showing you my dedication to you as a husband."

Georgia could not help but be touched by his speech and felt her heart lighten. Gratitude filled her mind and gradually tipped the scale of her decision.

"I came early with the sole, selfish purpose of begging an answer out of you," he continued. "It perhaps may seem cruel to force a reply, but, though I am a vicar, I am still a man with faults and imperfections. Our acquaintance has been short, yes, but if you prefer to wait a year to wed, then I shall wait to wed."

Georgia felt herself wanting to laugh, but quickly suppressed it. She could not, however, stop herself from taking this opportunity to tease him. "You cannot wait a few days for an answer, but you can wait a year to marry?" she asked with a smirk.

Mr. Janes blushed slightly but smiled. "I confess, it sounds contradictory, but I promise if you wish to wait a year to wed, then I shall never pressure you to do otherwise."

Georgia looked down at the ground for a moment before taking a deep breath and looking up at him. "Yes," she said as she breathed out.

At first, Mr. Janes must not have heard her, or did not believe what he had heard because he merely stood there looking dumbstruck.

Georgia blinked at him. "Mr. Janes? I-I accept. I will be your wife," she said, bringing a smile to his face.

"You will?" he repeated in mild bewilderment.

She smiled softly and nodded. "Yes."

Mr. Janes took her hands joyously in his and pressed them to his lips. "What a blessed day this is!" he proclaimed.

Georgia continued to smile as Mr. Janes continued to profess his happiness. She could not say that she was overflowing with joy as Mr. Janes appeared to be, but she was not unhappy. In fact, part of her was glad that she had found herself a different prospect from what she thought she would be. Being a married woman would certainly give her sister one less thing to laugh at than if she were to become an old maid.

She knew she should feel bad for only saying yes as a means to get out of a less appealing situation, but she did not. She wanted a life of happiness shared with the man she loved and their children. She might not have secured the man she loved, but at least her prospect of having children of her own had improved. Her own household, a modicum of independence. She respected Mr. Janes, and more importantly, he seemed to respect and care for her. She told herself that was enough and she was starting to believe it.

"Tell me, my dear," Mr. Janes said, breaking her from her thoughts, "when shall we wed? When shall we become one in the eyes of God?"

Georgia slightly blanched at the phrasing but soon regained herself. "Why do we not wed a year from today?" she asked. "I believe that should satisfy us both."

"A year from today," he sighed happily. "A day that could never have brought me more joy. Your birthday, our engagement, and soon, our wedding." He nodded satisfactorily. "So it shall be."

"We should return," Georgia told him. "I am sure the other guests will be arriving soon, and I need to dress for dinner."

"Yes, yes, of course!" he exclaimed gently taking her arm under his. "Shall we announce our joy tonight? Shall you allow me to tell those dearest to us that you soon shall be Mrs. Janes?"

She slowly nodded in agreement. It was best to get certain things over with sooner rather than later. "Yes, if it will please you," she replied.

"But will it please you, my gem?"

Georgia baulked a little at this term of endearment; it sounded strange to her ears. "It will please me for you to announce it, but not until after supper."

This satisfied Mr. Janes and upon entering the house, they parted. Georgia rushed to her bedroom; her stomach twisted in knots. She paced the room, wringing her hands and shaking her head. She wanted to take it back; she wanted to go back and say no. But she could not. It was already done. And it was done for the best. Perhaps, Louisa was right, and she would learn to love Mr. Janes. She already respected him and that was a step in the right direction, was it not?

GEORGIA FIDGETED AS SHE SAT IN THE PARLOR WAITING FOR THE other guests to arrive. She was mildly embarrassed at the prospect of hers and Mr. Janes' announcement. The thought of everyone congratulating her and making a fuss made her blush over and over.

Everyone would already be there to celebrate her, but this just gave them another reason to do so. She abhorred being the center of attention. At first, the idea of the announcement seemed harmless, but as the time went by, and the more she thought of it, Georgia began to break out into a sweat.

What would Mr. Garrett think? was a thought that passed through her mind more than once. *What would it matter?* was another.

Still, her heart beat wildly in her chest as the time drew nearer for the guests to arrive. She knew she should be bursting with joy, but instead she felt she should burst into tears.

Mr. Janes on the other hand, was calm and cheerful. He talked energetically to Mr. Barker and Louisa about how he wished to plant apple trees in the following spring and expand his library. He smiled and nodded like the day was any other day, inwardly counting the minutes until he could tell of his happy news.

Finally, Mr. Garrett arrived, and Georgia felt as if she could finally breathe. She let out a sigh of relief as he was introduced and he quickly walked over to her, bowing.

"I congratulate you on your birthday," Mr. Garrett said to her. "And I must beg your forgiveness for the other day. I do not know what I would have done if something worse had happened to you. I would never forgive myself. I did come to inquire about you yesterday but was told you were resting. Though I left reassured that you were much better."

Georgia smiled with warmth and feeling. "Thank you for the birthday wishes," she replied. "And you do not have to feel bad for what happened. It was not your fault. I assure you there is nothing to forgive. I was only glad that you had not been hurt as well."

"You saying that does make me feel somewhat better," Mr. Garrett told her. "Me not having been hurt while you laid unconscious on the road made it all the worse. However, I cannot help but feel somewhat responsible."

She pressed her lips together to suppress a smirk. "If that is how you must feel, then I shall certainly lay some of the blame on you." She lifted her chin and narrowed her eyes playfully at him. "How dare you let that wretch of a creature snap at the horse and how dare you allow the horse to become so frightened by the beast! For shame, Mr. Garrett!"

He laughed through his nose.

"There. Are you satisfied?" she teased. "Have I done your guilty feelings justice?"

"Yes, and now they can soon be done away with."

He smiled at her so warmly that she had to look away as she was overcome by embarrassment and something much like regret.

He cleared his throat after a moment. "I brought you a small gift," he said pulling a parcel out of his jacket.

Georgia took the gift tentatively, her skin tingling with the warmth of their proximity. "You did not have to give me anything, Mr. Garrett," she whispered. "I am sure I told you as much the other day."

"I know," he replied with a nod, "but I wanted to."

Georgia's stomach fluttered and her cheeks flushed, but not in the same way they had been, not the way they did when she thought of announcing her engagement. This was not the flush of embarrassment.

"I *had* gone to the bookstore to try and find something for you there, but I thought all the books deficient of the wit you deserve. So I settled on something else in the hope it shall help you find the words you are searching for to start your next novel."

Georgia looked up at him in surprise.

"Go on. Open it," he gently urged.

Georgia carefully unwrapped the parchment paper and pulled out a peacock feather quill with a golden tip. She gaped at the gift, unable to say anything for several moments. "Mr. Garrett," she breathed, "it is too much."

"You do not like it?"

She shook her head, struggling for a second to find the words to speak. "I love it. It is beyond beautiful, but it is too much."

"I do not believe so. I believe it to be just enough, and I hope should go perfectly with your journal."

Georgia looked at him half bewildered. "Thank you."

"Now, you must not thank me too much." He smiled. "This gift is partially selfish."

Georgia's face lit up with his tone. "Is it?"

Mr. Garrett nodded. "I am waiting for a new novel from the illustrious Lady H and was hoping this might be the tool with which she writes it."

She laughed gently. "I do not know about illustrious, but I would hate to disappoint my fans."

He creased his brows and looked down for a moment before catching her gaze again. "You *are* illustrious, Lady H." He moved his hand so that the back of his knuckles brushed against hers.

Georgia's breath caught in her throat as she stared up at Mr. Garrett, the light from the candles dancing in his eyes. Her cheeks burned as the rest of the room fell silent around them. Mr. Garrett gently squeezed her hand, delicately running his thumb across her palm.

"What is that, Georgia?" Louisa asked coming over, causing Mr. Garrett to take a step back and breaking the spell between them.

Georgia cleared her throat, overcome with confusion. "It-it is a, uh, gift from Mr. Garrett for my birthday."

Louisa's eyes widened as she saw it. "How beautiful. That is very generous of you, Mr. Garrett." She looked from Mr. Garrett to Georgia.

Georgia nodded, her cheeks still flushed.

"It is nothing," Mr. Garrett said softly. After a moment, he bowed, offering Georgia another congratulations and walked off toward the other men in the room.

Louisa regarded her friend. "Georgia," she whispered, "what is the nature of yours and Mr. Garrett's relationship?"

Georgia frowned at her. "Have you not already asked me this?"

she retorted a little angry. "Mr. Garrett and I are friends."

Louisa pressed her lips together for a second, rubbing them together. "I had not mentioned this before, but I received a letter from Marcia a few weeks before you came."

"She has told you she is with child then? I was so happy to see her," Georgia quickly replied, happy to change the subject.

Louisa bobbed her head as she spoke. "Yes, she told me of her condition. She also informed me she caught you flirting with a handsome young man whose name she could not recall at the time she wrote the letter."

Georgia blushed and looked surprised. "I wonder whom she could be talking about," she remarked. "I do not recall ever flirting with anyone. I certainly do not recall doing so in front of Marcia."

Louisa looked over at Mr. Garrett. "Was Mr. Garrett with you when you saw Marcia?" she inquired.

"Yes, he was. I introduced them."

Louisa looked at her friend. "Georgia, are you in love with him?"

Georgia's breath stopped in her chest as she gasped, her heart pounding and skin prickling at the thought.

"Are you in love with Mr. Garrett?"

"N-no, do not be ridiculous. I could never—because he would never—" Georgia stopped herself as tears formed in her eyes. She quickly looked up and blinked them away.

Louisa took her friend's hand and squeezed it. "Then this is the reason you hesitated answering Mr. Janes! You are in love with Mr. Garrett," she exclaimed happily. "Thankfully, you have not given him an answer. Oh, you and Mr. Garrett together would be a wonderful match! Your wit and his easiness of manner!"

Georgia turned her head in her friend's direction and shook it. "It is already too late," she whispered as a tear fell.

Louisa put her arm around her friend and turned her away from the others. "You can break it off," she urged. "You can tell Mr. Janes you made a mistake."

Georgia shook her head again. "You do not understand, Louisa," she told her. "Mr. Garrett is in love with Evangelina. He does not want me. How could he when she is so beautiful and elegant and I am none of those things?" She removed her glasses from her face so she could easily wipe away her tears.

Louisa shook her head. "Evangelina is pretty, yes, but close your eyes to her and you will see her for what she is. A spoiled brat without an opinion of her own. That is not the kind of woman Mr. Garrett could ever love."

Georgia sighed. "I heard him. He told me so himself, Louisa. I am nothing to him."

"Does that journal look like nothing to you? Does that quill look like nothing to you?" She took her friend's hand. "You are looking in the wrong places."

"Please, stop filling my head with what cannot be, Louisa. Beauty does matter. Mr. Henry taught me that. My wit is estimable, perhaps even amusing, but it is not loveable."

Louisa gaped at her friend. "So what will you do then? Nothing?"

She took a deep breath and cleared her throat. "I will survive this as I always have."

Louisa shook her head. "You will survive? That is no way to live, Georgia."

Georgia licked her lips and smiled, pinching her cheeks to return color to them. "And, yet, it is how I have lived and will continue to do so."

Mr. Stokes and a few other guests were soon announced followed by Mrs. Janes who all shuffled their way in. They congratulated Georgia on her birthday, happy to have something to celebrate in their small circle.

Mrs. Janes smiled at her affectionately. "Oh, to be young again," she proclaimed, patting the younger woman's arm.

Georgia smiled glad for a change in subject. "To be young and ridiculous again?" She shook her head. "I prefer wisdom over the years of ignorance."

"Careful what you wish for, my dear," Mrs. Janes warned with a crooked smile. "Your youth will creep away before you know it. Before too long you will wake up with pains you had never had before. Your whole body creaking in ways you've never heard before."

Georgia laughed lightly. "Getting old is better than the alternative though, would you not say?"

The elder woman's smile broadened. "Yes, it is certainly better than that." She pulled a small, round tin out of her purse and handed it to Georgia. "I made you this for your birthday," she said.

"Oh," Georgia gently exclaimed, taking the proffered tin. "You did not have to give me anything.

The old woman nodded at her gift. "It is but a mere trifle. Go on! Open it. You shall see."

Georgia opened it and smiled. She gently pulled out a small satchel filled with herbs. She inhaled its spicy aroma and sighed satisfactorily before placing it back in the tin with the others.

"It is tea I have made from some of the herbs we collected," Mrs. Janes explained. "It is of my own making and is perfect for chill autumn evenings."

"That was very thoughtful of you," Georgia replied with feeling. "Thank you."

"Perhaps I will share the recipe with you one day."

Georgia blushed at her last remark but remained smiling.

Mr. Stokes approached her soon after and lifted his glass to her. "Congratulations, Miss Hamilton," he said with a slight bow. "I shall owe you a dance later."

Georgia stifled a laugh. "Thank you, sir, but I am in no need of gifts."

He waved her comment away. "I insist. It is the least I can do."

Georgia was saved from replying by dinner being announced but was obliged to be escorted by Mr. Stokes as he offered her his arm.

Chatter drifted down the table, mixing with the sounds of cutlery on plates and the clinking of glasses on the table. Throughout it all, there was an appearance of happiness as everyone smiled while they ate and drank, lifting their glasses to Georgia.

When the food was done being served, Mr. Janes flashed Georgia an inquiring look and she nodded in response, her stomach dropping. He stood slowly and lifted a glass, clearing his throat for everyone's attention.

"Good evening, everyone," he began unnecessarily. "As you all know, we are here to celebrate Miss Hamilton on her day of birth, a day when God blessed the world with a bright mind and gentle heart."

Georgia shifted uncomfortably where she sat, trying to keep a smile on her face.

"It has been a joy meeting her and getting to know her. I hope we shall take this night to be grateful that we have been graced with her presence. And, I, well, I have even more to celebrate, as it is with a light, joyous heart that I announce Miss Hamilton's and my engagement."

He held out his hand for Georgia who slowly rose, smiling as the congratulations flowed from everyone. For a moment, she even ventured to look at Mr. Garrett whose face she could not decipher. It was Mrs. Janes who made the most of the announcement. She stood from her seat and took Georgia by the hands, kissing her on both cheeks.

"I shall finally have a daughter," she said happily.

Georgia, though silent, smiled at her future mother-in-law, accepting all her good wishes and pats on the cheek.

The rest of the night was a blur. It was almost as if Georgia was in a daydream as she sat and smiled and thanked everyone for their kind words. She accepted their praise and congratulations, answering questions the best she could.

She barely even noticed when Mr. Garrett left before the card tables were drawn.

23

A couple of days later, while Georgia was writing her father after church, Mr. Garrett called. He looked rather ashamed at finding her alone, avoiding her gaze when he first entered the room.

"It seems you have a habit of interrupting my letters," Georgia lightly teased.

"Forgive me," he quickly apologized. "I did not mean to disrupt your thoughts."

She laughed softly. "There is nothing to forgive; I was merely joking."

He nodded and shifted uncomfortably where he stood. "I do not think I formally congratulated you on your engagement."

Georgia's stomach flipped forgetting for a moment her situation.

"I wish you and Mr. Janes all the happiness."

She blushed and looked away. "Thank you."

"Perhaps now you can have something to write about."

"What?" She glanced back at him, confused.

"Your journal," he reminded her. "Perhaps this could be your story."

"Oh," she replied with a small nod. "I suppose it could."

There was an awkward pause between them.

"Is Barker home?" Mr. Garrett finally asked, breaking the silence.

She nodded. "I believe he is in his study, yes. Are you to stay for dinner?" she quickly added, not wanting him to leave the room.

He shook his head. "No, I came to say good-bye. I am taking my leave tomorrow."

"Oh, I thought you had more business here. Is there not more to do with your property? I thought there were more plans to go over."

He shook his head. "Nothing Barker could not handle without me," he told her. "Everything else I can communicate by letter."

She nodded again, stiffly. "Are you to finish the season out in

Barchester then?" she asked, thinking of all she could to engage him in further conversation.

Mr. Garrett pressed his lips together and shook his head. "No, I believe I must return to Cornwall. I will spend a few days more at my aunt's and then I will move on from there."

Georgia smiled weakly. "You will be stopping by there then?"

He nodded absently. "I have some things to settle there before I continue on."

Georgia felt herself blanch.

Was he going there to propose to Evangelina?

She quickly blinked back the tears that threatened to glisten in her eyes, preventing her from saying anything else.

"I shall let you get back to your letter, then," he said with a bow after a few moments' hesitation. "Good-bye, Miss Hamilton."

"Good-bye, Mr. Garrett," she replied solemnly as she watched him leave the room. She plopped down on one of the sofas, her heart feeling heavy and her chest tight. She pressed her hand over her heart and breathed in and out, trying to relieve the pressure. Hot tears welled in her eyes, but she refused to let them fall, quickly wiping them away before they could.

This was how Louisa found her a few minutes later. She rushed to her friend's side to comfort her, gently rubbing her back.

"I should not have pressured you into accepting Mr. Janes," she said. "Had I had any inkling you loved Mr.—"

"Please, do not say his name," Georgia stopped her, sniffing. "It would not have mattered anyways. I would have accepted Mr. Janes regardless. It is unlikely- improbable actually- that I would ever receive another offer of marriage again. I certainly never would have received one from *him*." She closed her eyes and drew a shaky breath. "Do you think less of me for doing so?"

Louisa shook her head. "I cannot blame you for wanting what you want."

"But you *can* blame me for how I go about getting it," Georgia concluded. "That is just as well. I can blame myself for it. Mr. Janes, however, is a good man and I believe in time my respect for him could grow into something more."

Louisa rubbed her arm. "Things will sort themselves out," she reassured her. "Come, we should eat some lunch."

The women rose and made their way to the door when a servant rushed in with a letter.

"This come for Miss 'amilton, ma'am," he said, handing it to her with a bow. "It come by express."

The women exchanged glances as Georgia took the letter and thanked the young man. "It is from my father," she said tearing the seal and opening it. She scanned through its contents and gasped, reaching for a chair for support.

Louisa took her by the arm to steady her. "What is it?" she asked, alarmed, helping her down into a chair.

She sat shakily. "It is Evangelina," she replied breathlessly, pressing a hand to her mouth.

"Well, is she alright?" Louisa pressed when she did not continue.

"She—she—she has fallen prey to Mr. Talbot," Georgia stuttered. "She has given herself to him."

"What? Who?"

Georgia handed her the letter. "Please read it!" she half shouted. "It is more than I can comprehend."

Louisa took the letter, reading with her eyes wide.

My dearest girl,

I know you might be alarmed at the mode in which this letter was delivered, but rest assured, we are well. This letter is to inform you of some terrible news that will no doubt reach you soon enough and I wanted to be the one to tell you.

Your sister, who for several months, unbeknownst to us, has been courted by a worthless man of worthless character. He has seduced her and left her in the wind. In her desperation, she continued to try to pursue him only for him to publicly denounce her. This despicable creature- this honor-less man is Vince Talbot.

Your mother is beside herself and your sister has not left her room for shame.

It is with a heavy heart I tell you this as it is very likely to ruin any of your future prospects. I ask that you return home as soon as possible. I am sorry to cut your visit with Louisa short, but I must have you home. I am all out of wisdom and I am afraid my anger will distort my abilities to make the right decisions.

> *Your ever-loving father*

"Oh, Georgia, I shall ready the carriage immediately," Louisa told her. "I shall have a servant pack our things!"

"Our?" Georgia asked.

"Surely I cannot let you travel so far alone in the state you are in," Louisa told her. "No, I shall go with you. I will inform the staff of what we need, and I shall tell Gregory you must be rushed home due to a family emergency."

"You will not tell him yet what has happened?" Georgia begged.

Louisa shook her head. "No, I will be discreet if you wish, but as he is my husband, I will eventually have to tell him."

She nodded. "Then tell him now," she replied softly. "It is better that way. But—" she paused, "but perhaps you could tell him not within Mr. Garrett's presence. I will write to him later, but do not let him find out today."

Louisa squeezed her friend's hand and rushed out of the room, leaving Georgia to her tears.

The two women were gone within the hour. Georgia, despite her emotional exhaustion, stared out the window of the carriage as it pulled along. Her poor sister was all she could think about. Used and thrown away by the man she had loved. She felt for her, and she blamed herself.

She knew it was not a rational feeling. She could never have predicted what was going to happen, but she saw the impropriety of her attentions toward Mr. Talbot. She saw the flirtations and felt the tension between them. She witnessed the verbal altercation between the two and had done nothing to further guide her sister.

She shook her head. What would it have mattered? She had already confronted Evangelina about Mr. Talbot and his attentions toward her, and she did nothing but laugh at her in return. Would it have made a difference if she had informed her parents about them?

"I am sorry for what your sister is going through," Louisa said, seeing the torment in her friend's eyes. "I know this is not good."

Georgia took in a deep breath and let it out slowly. "I will have to inform Mr. Janes of what happened," she replied looking over at her. "He will break off the engagement, no doubt."

Louisa shook her head. "You cannot be sure of that."

Georgia nodded. "He is a vicar," she pointed out. "He cannot marry a woman whose sister lost herself to immoral temptation. What kind of message would that send to all of his parishioners?"

Louisa huffed angrily. "Why is it that your sister has to ruin everything for you? None of this would have happened if your mother had stayed out of things and had not—" She stopped herself and turned her head to avoid Georgia's gaze.

"If my mother had not what?" Georgia asked, frowning.

"I should not have said anything."

"Louisa," Georgia said in a stern tone. "What did my mother do?"

Louisa took a deep breath and let it out slowly. "I promised Ross that I would not tell you, but I think you should know." She paused for a moment to gather her thoughts. "Ross proposed to your sister last April, right after her eighteenth birthday. And she accepted him."

Georgia blinked at her friend in disbelief.

"Your mother, however, did not. She persuaded Evangelina she was meant for a greater, better man than my brother and convinced her to break it off. She turned your sister against my brother as if he were beneath her notice. Perhaps if your mother had not unwantedly meddled, your sister would not have disgraced herself and you."

"But," she shook her head, confused and a little hurt, "why would you have not told me? I would have brought the matter to Papa who adores Ross as his own son. He would have been elated at the prospect of joining our two houses!"

"Ross did not want you to get involved," Louisa told her. "He wanted Evangelina to make the choice to disobey your mother on her own. He also did not want you to think too poorly on your mother."

Georgia let out a small moan. "Oh, the pain Ross must have been feeling this past year and I had teased him for it, not knowing the true pain I was causing him. I have been an awful friend to him."

"You could not have known," Louisa reassured her.

Georgia dabbed at her tears. "My family is sure to be ruined soon enough, in more ways than one. Neither of us shall marry nor could we ever hope to gain appointments as governesses. Who would want a young woman teaching their children about morality when she herself gives into temptation? And I shall be cast into the lot with her." Her chest ached with the anxiety of what this meant for her family as the carriage prattled along too slowly for her growing impatience.

24

Georgia and Louisa arrived just after nine in the evening. They were welcomed with great enthusiasm by Mr. Hamilton and with a skeptical eye from his wife who was not sure what Georgia needed to be there for; she thought even less of Louisa's presence.

"Where is Lina?" Georgia asked.

"In her room where she belongs," her mother replied a little coldly. "Hopefully thinking of what she has done to her family."

Her father looked at her, an ashamed look on his face. "You should go up and talk to her," he urged gently.

Georgia nodded, shooting Louisa a glance before she made her way up to her sister's bedroom. She knocked when she came to the door and listened. When there wasn't an answer, she called out, letting her sister know it was her.

A few moments later, she heard the lock turn, and her sister opened the door looking disheveled, her eyes puffy. "What on earth are you doing here?" she sniffed. "You are supposed to be at Louisa's."

Georgia smiled somberly and nodded. "I was," she replied slipping through the door. "But I heard you were in need of comfort, and I came directly."

Evangelina swallowed a sob as she moved back to her bed and fell on it. "Oh, Georgia! What have I done?" she wailed.

Georgia went over to her sister and sat on the bed next to her. "Tell me what happened." She placed her hand gently on her sister's back, the tenderness of the gesture causing her sister to convulse with sobs.

Evangelina sniffed after a minute, trying to catch her breath. "I cannot!" she proclaimed. "Do not make me relive my agony!"

Georgia sighed patiently. "I understand the pain and humiliation you must feel- what feelings this circumstance has brought- but holding them in will not make you feel better. Hiding your shame will never help you come to terms with it- own it."

Evangelina slowly turned her head to look at her sister.

"I know. You must think it ridiculous for me to be telling you to share your feelings seeing as I very rarely ever do. However, I have learned recently that it is sometimes safer to share what you feel than to hide it away. Not communicating something so easy as a feeling can lead to confusion and even greater heartache than you had before."

Evangelina sniffed and blinked at her sister, unsure of her motives.

"Do not look so uneasy," Georgia softly told her. "I am not here to judge, but to listen. I offer nothing except to hear your side of the story and to comfort you the way only a sister can." She smiled at her reassuringly.

After a few more moments' hesitancy, Evangelina nodded. "It happened at the Hayes little dinner party the day we walked there with Mr. Garrett. Mr. Talbot had been promising to take me away from here. He promised me a dazzling life in town with dinner parties, theater visits, walks in the park along the lake, and balls. He promised long visits to Bath and Lyme and the continent just the two of us. He had promised such beautiful things. Things we would share together. He talked of traveling, seeing the world, sharing our very souls with one another." She paused as she crawled to the head of her bed and propped herself up on the pillows. "He told me that he loved me and wanted to spend the rest of our lives together.

"After dinner, he said he would escort me home. We shared the Hayes' carriage where he continued to whisper such lovely tales in my ear." She shivered as she remembered the feel of his breath on her skin. "I had had a few more drinks than I had ought, and he kissed me and then again, and then his kisses turned into caresses. Before I knew it, he was moving his hands up my skirts and—" She stopped herself as she began to sob again. "I believed him! He had painted such a beautiful picture of what life could have been if the two of us could just be together and I bought it! I am such a fool!"

Georgia shushed her gently.

"And then after, he began avoiding me," Evangelina continued. "He would refuse to talk to me or even look at me when we were at the same gathering. I could not take it anymore, so Friday evening, at the Bourghs', I confronted him. I asked him why he had been acting so cruel to me and in front of everyone he said- he said," she inhaled sharply, "he said he did not associate with sluts that so easily give themselves to men with whom they are not wed. He then laughed at me as if I were a joke, as if I were nothing!" She buried her face in her hands again and sobbed.

"Oh, Evangelina, how awful."

"The whole party must have heard it and if they had not, by the end of the night the scene had been replayed to them by someone who had." She shook her head. "I have been utterly mortified. Ruined!"

"And what of your monthly courses?" Georgia asked anxiously.

Her sister looked a little abashed at the question. "I have had them since. I am not with child. But it does not matter. My shame cannot be abated."

"You made a mistake," Georgia replied in a soft tone. "You are hardly the first woman to do so. People love to judge what they do not understand, and I am sure there are some among them that have committed the same act. They are just allowed to be cruel because they were not caught."

Fresh tears streamed down Evangelina's face as she stared at her sister in disbelief. "Why are you being so nice to me?" She took in a ragged breath, her chest quivering as she exhaled.

Georgia frowned at her. "Because you are my sister," she replied matter-of-factly. "Am I not supposed to be nice to you? To look after you?"

Evangelina sobbed harder. "Even after how I have always treated you?" she said almost inaudibly. "You still have it in you to be kind to me after my failings? After I have ruined the both of us?"

Georgia pulled her sister to her, wrapping her arms around her tightly. "Even after everything," she whispered, planting a kiss on her forehead. "None of that matters when you are in need. We are family and sometimes," she paused, "sometimes family is all we have."

Evangelina settled in her sister's arms, sniffling. "I love you, Georgia," she whispered.

Georgia smiled. "I love you, too."

"You love me despite it all? Even though I have ruined everything for us?" she asked tentatively. "Even though our chances of regaining our fortune are lost because of what I have done?"

Georgia gently pushed her sister away and took her face in her hands. "Until my dying breath," she reassured her.

Evangelina managed a smile. "Mamma is furious with me, is she not?"

Georgia let a sigh escape her as she dropped her hands from her sister's face. "Mamma is disappointed that her plans for you will not come into fruition," she began gingerly, "but mamma has always been easily disappointed. I would not fret over it."

Evangelina shook her head. "This is different," she told her. "This is more than being upset over not being able to go to town, or papa refusing to throw a ball. This is bigger than that. I allowed myself to get lost in my fancy for an underserving man and, now- oh, Georgia, I will die alone because of it!"

"You cannot think that to be true," Georgia soothed. "One day, you will find a man worthy of your love and if he loves you in return, he should not care about your past transgressions."

"But that is all men care about," Evangelina surmised. "Past trans-gressions. I am impure and, therefore, undesirable."

Georgia shifted her gaze to her hands, frowning slightly. "What about Ross?" she asked after a moment, looking back up at Evangelina.

Even in the fading light from the fireplace, Georgia could see her sister blanche.

"What about him?"

"Why did you not tell me about the two of you?" Georgia asked.

"What do you mean?"

"He had proposed to you."

Evangelina looked away. "Please, I do not want to talk about it."

Georgia nodded. "I understand that it might hurt, but do you think he will turn away like all of the others?"

Evangelina's lips began to tremble again. "Why should he not? What about Ross would be any different than anyone else?"

Georgia furrowed her brows. "Because he loves you still, Lina." She reached out and took her sister's hand. "Have you honestly not seen it? The look in his eyes every time you meet?"

Evangelina pressed her free hand to her mouth to suppress another sob. She shook her head. "No, I have given up on Ross. I was *made* to give him up."

Georgia pressed a hand to Evangelina's cheek. "But he has not given up on you," she replied tenderly. "He *loves* you."

"What left do I have to love?" Evangelina asked her. "The person he fell in love with no longer exists. I have been cruel and have in return been treated cruelly. Perhaps, this is the fate I deserve."

Georgia took her sister's hand and squeezed it. "No, I do not and cannot believe that," she told her with conviction.

Evangelina shook her head. "I can," she said. "I gave up my chances to be with Ross. I turned him away, shunned him, ignored him. Why—how could I ever expect a return of his affections?"

"Do you still love him?"

Evangelina pressed her eyes shut and took a deep breath through her nose. "I—I do not know. Mamma convinced me that I did not. She told me my feelings for him were based on the fond memories he and I shared as children. She convinced me that I was too young to know what was good for me much less what love was." She shook her head. "Perhaps she is right; I do not know what love is at all. I fancied myself in love with—with *that man* and look where it has gotten me. I do not know what love is, so I do not know if I still love Ross."

Georgia nodded. "Perhaps no one truly knows," she said quietly, patting her sister's hand. "Perhaps everyone has their own ideas of what love is and do not realize that love has a different meaning for one person than it does for another."

Evangelina laughingly huffed. "You always say things like that, Georgia," she pointed out.

Georgia creased her brow. "Like what?"

Evangelina shook her head briefly. "Things that make complete sense yet no sense at all."

Georgia smirked. "I do not think *that* makes any sense."

Evangelina smiled back at her though solemnly. "I am sorry if I ruined your prospects of marriage."

Georgia looked confused.

"I saw that man who came to talk to papa," she explained. "I listened at the door."

Georgia patted her hand. "We shall see. I have yet to tell him, but this is not something I can avoid."

Evangelina nodded.

Georgia leaned in and kissed her sister on the forehead. "I expect you at breakfast tomorrow," she told her firmly, yet, gently as she stood from the bed. "It is one thing to be ashamed of what you have done; it is another to take responsibility for it. You cannot wallow in self-pity the rest of your life."

Evangelina bowed her head, but Georgia gently lifted her chin.

"We will get through this one day at a time. Together."

Her sister nodded again, a small smile spreading across her lips. "Thank you, Georgia, for everything."

Georgia smiled at her. "Good night, Lina." She planted another kiss on her sister's forehead and left the room.

Evangelina did in fact come downstairs to breakfast the following morning. Though she held her head high, her eyes reflected the shame she felt for her actions. Before sitting with her family, she formally apologized, saying how she hoped to make them all amends.

Her mother only looked up at her to scowl, and opened her mouth to comment when her husband reached over and took her by the hand. He looked at his wife sternly, silencing her before inviting his youngest daughter to sit.

It had been awkward as no one knew what to say, nor did any of them want to be the first to speak, but it was a start to patching up what had been broken between them with each morning getting better. Soon enough, conversation flowed more easily and readily between them all with even Mrs. Hamilton's scowls becoming less frequent. After a week, there was even some laughter.

25

The morning after her arrival, Georgia decided she should inform Mr. Janes about her sister's situation. It was inevitable that he was to find out sooner or later in some fashion and it would pain her to think someone other than herself told him.

She explained the situation with gravity, telling him she understood if they could no longer continue their engagement as his profession had certain expectations from his wife and her family. For the sake of what honor she might have left, she, if he agreed, would rescind her acceptance of his proposal.

It was not a long letter, but it was written with feeling and without shame or anxiety. It was quickly drawn out, folded and sealed and sent on its way. Within a couple of days, she received a response, and it was the response she had expected.

Mr. Janes, as devasted as he felt, agreed with her repeal. Though he did not doubt her purity and morality, he could not in good conscience marry a woman whose sister exhibited salacious behavior. He then wished her well, noting that he would pray for her and for her family.

It was not a letter that particularly brought her joy or pain, but she was surprised that it brought her relief. Evangelina's mistake certainly ruined her only hopes of marrying, but it also saved her from an unhappy marriage, and she could not be angry with that.

She folded the letter and threw it in the fire soon after reading it, watching it curl and crackle in the flames before it was consumed and disappeared into ash.

"I suppose you will no longer be able to make your appointment," her mother said bitterly, walking into the parlor.

"I suppose I will not," Georgia answered without looking at her.

"We are in a very big mess, Georgia," her mother continued. "We have already had to sell some of our possessions, including my favorite carriage. Dresses that I had ordered from town to be made were canceled and I have had to beg my brother for a loan. She huffed. "I am sure he is satisfied with it too. I could all but see the sneer on his face when I read his letter acquiescing to our request. Hateful man never had a nice word to say about anybody and he never approved of your father." She lifted a brow. "Though now I might see why."

Georgia frowned and her stomach curdled with anger.

Her mother waved her hand dismissively as she sat down in agitation. "Your sister has destroyed us by throwing herself into the arms of that man. I hope she is satisfied. Selfish girl."

"She did not throw herself into that man's arms, mamma," Georgia corrected. "You forced her into them."

Her mother gaped at her. "I beg your pardon?"

"Had you not interfered between her and Ross, she would never have aligned herself with someone as diabolical as Mr. Talbot," Georgia informed her. "In truth, she might already be married had it not been for your selfish, greedy schemes."

Mrs. Hamilton blanched. "I do not regret my decision for that," she said, standing proudly. "Ross is beneath her. She could have gotten someone worth three times as much and she almost did with Mr. Garrett."

Georgia shook her head. "Evangelina and Ross were in love, mamma, and you forbade them from being together."

"As a mother, you only want what is best for your children and Ross was not it."

"Best for your children, or best for you?" Georgia retorted. "Ross is a good, kind man. His fortune may not be as impressive as Mr. Garrett's, but he could have very well afforded Evangelina a comfortable life! Beyond that, he loved her! Cherished her! And because of *your* wants and *your* desires- nay- *your* selfishness, you tore them apart without caring about the consequences or the feelings of those involved!"

"Do not talk to me like that, Georgia," Mrs. Hamilton warned. "Regardless of how you feel, I am still your mother, and you will respect me."

"As my mother, I will," Georgia replied coldly. "But as a person, I do not have to, and I will not."

Her mother looked at her astonished and opened her mouth as if she wished to say something when the door to the room was opened and Mr. Garrett was introduced. Both of the women went pale for a moment before blushing in confusion.

"Mr. Garrett," Mrs. Hamilton said, regaining herself quicker than Georgia could. "What an unexpected, yet, welcome surprise."

"Forgive my intrusion," he replied with a bow.

"Intrusion?" Mrs. Hamilton repeated, feigning a laugh. "You could never intrude upon us, Mr. Garrett. You must know you are always welcome."

He nodded, venturing a look at Georgia who was unable to meet his eye.

"Shall I fetch Evangelina?" Mrs. Hamilton asked causing a flutter of pain throughout Georgia's chest.

"No, ma'am," Mr. Garrett quickly replied not breaking his gaze from Georgia. "I am here for Miss *Georgia* Hamilton."

Georgia flushed, feeling the heat spread throughout her body.

"Oh," Mrs. Hamilton uttered, not hiding the disappointment and confusion behind the word.

"Shall we walk, Miss Hamilton?" he asked her.

Georgia finally looked up at him but was unable to breathe.

"Georgia, my dear," her mother said with a constrained laugh when her daughter did not answer. "Mr. Garrett is talking to you."

"Yes," Georgia finally said barely above a whisper. "A walk would be lovely."

Mr. Garrett bowed and moved out of the room.

His movement was so sudden, it took Georgia by surprise and after shooting her mother a confused glance she followed him. Mr.

Garrett walked quickly, almost feverishly, and she felt as if she had to run to keep up with him. Once he finally rounded the corner of the house, however, he slowed down.

"Forgive me. My appearance here must be confusing to you," he finally said after Georgia caught up with him.

Georgia blinked at him for a moment almost out of breath. "I must confess that it is," she replied softly.

He nodded. "When my aunt informed me of your sister's situation at breakfast this morning, I had to confirm it myself, from you."

Georgia bobbed her head. "I am sorry you had to find out the way you did. I wanted to write you myself, but I lacked the courage. It is true, however. My sister made the mistake of taking a worthless man at his word and now she is ruined while he happily lives his life."

"I am sorry—very sorry to hear this."

Georgia nervously fidgeted with her glasses. "I am grateful for your concern."

He shook his head. "Again, I am sorry for my intrusion for I know it is not the time to receive visitors. The thought of it must be repugnant. But it pained me greatly when my aunt told me, and I could not bear to think what pain you and your family must be feeling yourselves."

"We are bearing it best we can," Georgia replied a little awkwardly. "Most of our neighbors have shunned us. Louisa is still visiting her parents and comes every other day, but I have yet to see Ross since I have returned, which I must confess has been disappointing. Louisa said he has business in town, though I am sure something as serious as this would—" She shook her head. "Never mind."

He nodded. "You have informed your fiancé?"

Georgia smiled somberly again. "Former fiancé," she corrected. "I received his letter just this morning. I suggested it would be best if we broke off our engagement and he agreed. As a vicar, I suppose I cannot blame him."

Mr. Garrett stopped walking and turned to her, a strange look of pain followed by a flash of something else sparkled in his eyes. "Miss Hamilton, if there were words that I could say to lessen the pain of such a disappointment, I would say them, but I do not believe they exist."

"Perhaps not," she sighed. "But the sentiment is felt just the same, Mr. Garret. Thank you."

He gave a small bow as they continued to walk.

"I am sorry for you as well, Mr. Garrett, and I understand if you would also prefer not to associate with us any longer."

He looked at her, confused. "Why would *you* feel sorry for me?" he asked.

She stammered for a moment. "Because you were in love with my sister," she replied slowly. "And have now learned how unworthy she was of your affections."

He regarded her for a moment before laughing.

Georgia readjusted her glasses, frowning. "I do not see what is so funny."

"I cannot understand it. Why is it that everyone thinks I am in love with your sister?" he asked, still laughing.

"Are you not?" Georgia replied, bewildered. "You confessed it the other day in the phaeton."

"I did no such thing." He shook his head fervently. "No, to be honest, as much as I respect your sister, talking to her is like talking to a wall. A vain, pretty wall, but a wall nonetheless."

Georgia laughed lightly though confused. "Then all of those times you came to visit her, meant nothing?" she inquired, still not convinced.

Mr. Garrett took in a deep breath and let it out slowly. "Miss Hamilton, I never came to visit your sister," he informed her. "I came all those times for you. Your sister's presence was merely forced upon me."

Georgia looked away, blinking away the fog as she remembered all of his visits and how readily her mother was to suggest that he and

Evangelina take a walk, or take a ride together, or take tea with them. He was right. Barely would he have been introduced to the room when her mother would push Evangelina in his way.

She shook her head in disbelief. "You only came to visit me?"

He nodded. "I tried to make my feelings known on more than one occasion, but it was difficult getting anyone to let me have a word in otherwise and my shy nature made it difficult for me to correct them."

"Feelings?" she asked, blinking, her head swimming with a thousand questions. "I do not understand you. You came for me and not my sister? But- but everyone comes to visit Evangelina."

"I understand your hesitancy and disbelief," he began, "but my intentions were to get to know you better and as time wore on I- I was hoping to court you." He stopped walking again and faced her.

Georgia's breath caught in her throat as her entire body flushed. "What?" she replied in a hushed voice, her heart throbbing in her chest.

"Yes, perhaps, others do not look at you and see what they see in Evangelina. Her glowing skin and hair, her bright eyes and slight figure."

Georgia frowned and she pursed her lips to keep from saying anything. Her flush of confusion slowly turning to annoyance.

"But what I do *not* see when I look at your sister is a lifetime of laughter and happiness; I see a beauty that will wither away and a youthfulness that will fade; I see long nights filled with dull conversation and endless balls with shallow people in attendance; I see unfulfillment and stagnation." He took a step closer to her.

Georgia felt herself tremble as he spoke.

"That is not what I see when I look at you, however."

She exhaled shakily. "And what do you see?" she asked breathlessly.

Mr. Garrett slowly reached out and brushed his hand against hers, sending chills through them both. "I see a small cottage with a library where the books are stacked so high, they are a hazard to all who pass by them. I see long walks in the mornings and you writing throughout the day by an obnoxiously roaring fire surrounded by no less than three dogs."

Georgia took in a shaky breath.

"I see the love and life I have always wanted." He gently took her hand in his and brushed his thumb against it. "You may not be society's standard for beauty, but you are mine."

Georgia felt her heart swell in her chest, and she shook her head, unable to believe what she was hearing. "I do not understand. But you are always blushing around Evangelina."

Mr. Garrett let out a small huff. "Am I not allowed to blush if I am uncomfortable or embarrassed?" he retorted.

"Is not embarrassment a sign of love?" she inquired accussingly.

He gaped at her for a moment. "No," he breathed. "If you are in love with someone, what is there to be embarrassed or uncomfortable about? What shame does loving someone bring?"

"You are not in love with my sister then?" Georgia asked, wanting to hear him say it again.

Mr. Garrett shook his head with a laugh, pressing her hand. "Dearest Georgia, no," he answered softly, bringing her hand to his lips. "I am in love with you."

A small sob escaped Georgia's lips and she covered her mouth with her other hand to stifle it.

"And I must confess how selfish of a creature I am," he continued. "When you told me Mr. Janes agreed to break off your engagement, I felt elation. Yes, I was hurt for you, but for myself, I felt hope."

Georgia continued to cry.

"I am glad," Mr. Garrett said. "I am glad your engagement is over because now I can ask you for your hand."

Georgia felt her knees go weak as she collapsed to the ground.

"Miss Hamilton!" Mr. Garrett exclaimed, alarmed, kneeling in front of her. "Are you unwell?"

Georgia shook her head. "No," she replied, recollecting herself. "I am well." She wiped away her tears and began to laugh. "I am very well."

Mr. Garrett smiled at her.

"Tell me again," she said taking his hand and pressing it to her lips. "Please, say it again."

"I love you."

Georgia closed her eyes and smiled, shaking her head. "The last part."

"I want to ask you for your hand," he said grinning, "in marriage."

Georgia opened her eyes, her tears causing them to glisten. "Then go on," she finally said. "Ask!"

Mr. Garrett chuckled and stood, helping Georgia from the ground. "Miss Hamilton, Georgia, would you do me the great honor of becoming my wife?"

Georgia pressed her hands to her cheeks and nodded. "Yes!" she proclaimed with tears streaming down her face. "Oh, Mr. Garrett! Yes!"

Mr. Garrett laughed as he took Georgia's hands and kissed them again. "I have never felt happier than this moment."

"No one will believe us!" Georgia exclaimed with a laugh. "Everyone will be in such shock to hear it."

He shook his head. "I do not know why they should," he replied.

"Because everyone, including myself, thought you were in love with Evangelina," she explained. "Even the last time we met here, you were paying her an awful lot of attention."

He blushed. "If I am being honest, I only did so at your instructions, and perhaps, with the hope it would make you jealous."

Georgia was taken aback by this statement.

"It is beneath me, I know," he began, "but after the argument between us, I was angry. I did not think you liked me and thought that even you wanted me to be with your sister. So, I began to ask her to dance more and stood closer to her than usual."

"How awful you are!" she teased.

"It is terrible of me, I understand, but it taught me that there is much more to love about you than people give you credit for."

Georgia blushed and smiled. "How silly we have both been," she said sheepishly. "There you were loving me silently, while I was in denial about my love for you." She shook her head. "I told myself it could not be true, that you could never love me, so I forced myself to hide my feelings. But how could I not love you?" she continued with a sigh. "You are good and kind and thoughtful." She smirked and wrinkled her nose. "It does not hurt, however, that you are very handsome and conveniently wealthy."

Mr. Garrett laughed.

"Your perfect character is, therefore, complete!"

"I've no faults for you to point out?"

She thought for a moment. "Well, if that is where we want to begin our betrothal, then I would say your ears are slightly too small for your face."

"My ears?"

She gave a solitary nod. "Yes, that is all. For now, at least. I am sure I will come across the usual in time. You snore when you sleep, or slurp your wine distastefully, but why spoil the fun of finding that all out after we are wed?"

He laughed again, pressing her hands once more to his lips. "Should we not tell your family of our news? Or would you prefer to continue your examination of me?"

Georgia smiled broadly. "Oh, let us tell my family of our joy, that I, the elder sister, is to marry the illustriously handsome Mr. Garrett." She stifled a laugh. "I believe my mother might have an apoplexy when I tell her the news."

"I certainly hope not."

"No, no, I do not wish it, but she will be the hardest to convince of it."

He held out his arm which she took willingly. "Come then, let us inform your father first."

She nodded satisfactorily. "Yes, I like that idea. My father will at least do me justice and say he knew how it would be all along!"

26

THE SHOCK OF MISS GEORGIA HAMILTON'S ENGAGEMENT TO MR. Adam Garrett spread quickly throughout the town. At first, it was thought of as a joke. How could the handsome Mr. Garrett marry Miss Hamilton who was far from a beauty and was the non-beautiful sister of a ruined woman? But after it was confirmed by his Aunt and Uncle Dorset, the town grew silent on the subject as they truly did not know what to think.

The other single women and their families were disappointed. They had not had their fair shot at Mr. Garrett and for an entire month, every time Georgia stepped foot into town, she was met with looks of extreme jealously.

"Why her?" they would whisper.

"What has she done to deserve him?"

After a month, however, there was more interesting gossip to spread, and the town quickly lost interest in the couple. It had been heard that William Henry, the cousin of the Stanfords, was drunkenly walking along the side of the road when a carriage ran him over, killing him after three days of agonizing pain.

And Mr. Talbot? That was an even more interesting story. Mr. Talbot had been left on the streets of London badly beaten and missing three of his teeth. He survived, however, though his face would never be the same again.

"ROSS, WHAT AN UNEXPECTED SURPRISE!" GEORGIA EXCLAIMED entering the parlor and seeing Ross standing there looking out the window. Georgia gasped when she saw him. "What has happened to your face?"

Ross gently fingered a black eye and then his busted lip, the knuckles of his hand looking just as battered. "It is nothing," he reassured her. "I am fine."

Georgia regarded her friend for a moment. "What have you done, Ross?" she said in a stern tone. "You did not, did you?"

Ross stood straighter. "Did not what?"

She narrowed her eyes and took a few steps closer to him. "I heard what happened to Mr. Talbot."

Ross avoided her eye, clearing his throat. "I cannot for the life of me understand what you are talking about, Georgia."

Georgia let out a sigh. "Oh? Do you not?"

He shook his head, still avoiding her eye. "Not at all."

"Well, Mr. Talbot was attacked the other day."

"Was he? That is awful!"

"Mh." Georgia nodded. "He was beaten bloody and missing several of his teeth. He could barely speak when he was found."

"That sounds regrettable."

A smirk spread across her face. "For Mr. Talbot, I am sure it is."

"Do they have any idea who did it?"

Georgia shook her head. "No. Mr. Talbot says he cannot remember."

"How unfortunate."

She eyed her friend for a moment. "Yes, it is unfortunate, though I cannot say I feel sorry for him. Perhaps as a Christian I should, but as a mere human, I am pleased."

Ross smirked for a moment before clearing his throat again to hide his expression. "I came to congratulate you," he said. "Louisa told me about your engagement to Mr. Garrett."

Georgia blushed, grinning from ear to ear, and thanked him. "Yes, mamma is still in shock over it."

Ross chuckled. "I am sure she is, but I never doubted your ability to capture a man," he told her. "The right man had just not come along yet."

Georgia laughed quietly. "You know, as a friend you are indispensable."

He grinned. "I know." He nodded and looked down at the ground.

"I would have come sooner but I was," he paused, "in London on business."

"That is strange. That is where Mr. Talbot was attacked."

Ross shook his head. "Not so strange. London is full of dishonorable characters."

"Of course it is."

There was a brief silence.

"Did you want to see her?" Georgia asked.

Ross blanched. "Who?"

Georgia lifted a brow at him.

He looked away again. "I do not know," he replied, seeming torn. "I do not think I can."

Georgia frowned. "Then why have you come?"

"As I said, to congratulate you on your engagement," he tried confirming without conviction.

She shook her head. "No, you used that as an excuse to come here," she suspected. "Your real reason is something else."

Ross rubbed his mouth a little anxiously. "It is dangerous that you know me so well," he replied quietly.

"I can go and fetch her," Georgia told him.

"There is no need," came Evangelina's voice from the door. "I am already here."

All the color drained from Ross's face as he looked up at her, his anxiety melting away into something else, hope. Georgia recognized it immediately and, feeling herself the intruder, made her way to the door when Evangelina stopped her.

"No," her sister almost begged. "Please stay."

Georgia shot a glance at Ross who gave a small nod. She made her way to a chair and sat, though the scene was uncomfortable.

"What has happened to your face?" Evangelina asked sweetly.

Ross coughed. "Nothing," he replied. "It was an accident of sorts, but I am fine."

Evangelina looked unsure of his answer.

He smiled reassuringly and shook his head. "It is an awkward business, really. Not worth mentioning."

Georgia pressed her lips together to keep from saying anything.

Evangelina nodded as she came further into the room, twisting her hands nervously. "I wish to apologize to you, Ross," she began staring down at her hands.

He looked at her, his brows furrowed in confusion. "For what?"

"For all of the hurt I put you through," she replied slowly meeting his eye. "For allowing my mother to persuade me that I deserved better than you."

Ross looked away, a flash of anger in his eyes.

"But I learned too late that there is no one better than you," Evangelina continued, her eyes beginning to well up with tears.

Georgia's eyes grew wide with surprise and Ross looked back at Evangelina with astonishment.

"And I am sorry, more than I could ever express, that it took me this long to figure out my folly." Evangelina' s lip began to quiver as a tear fell. "That I had to go through all of this to make me see what I have given up. I was a fool."

Moved, Ross took a couple of steps toward her.

"I know what I have done has ruined me and I understand if you can no longer look at me as you once did, but I hope you and I could still remain friends. If you can promise me that, I could never wish for anything again."

"I love you," Ross blurted out without hesitation.

Evangelina let out a small gasp, while Georgia knew it was time for her to leave the room.

"What?" Evangelina breathed.

"I love you still," Ross continued. "I will always love you." He shook his head. "You know I am a man of my word and convictions. I am stubborn and moody and sometimes unbearable, I believe. But there is one thing I shall always be and that is constant in my love and regard for you."

"But what I have done- It is too much," Evangelina told him. "The world will never forgive me."

"Then the world be damned," Ross whispered.

Evangelina began to cry freely now as Ross took her hand and kissed it. Georgia used this as a distraction to quietly slip out of the room.

"Because I forgive you," was the last thing she heard as she closed the door.

"MR. FAIRGRAVE AND YOUR SISTER?" MR. GARRETT SAID LATER THAT afternoon.

Georgia nodded, smiling. "Yes!" she replied happily as they walked along the tree-lined lane. "He has been in love with her since she was fifteen."

"Oh."

She furrowed her brow. "Is something wrong?"

Mr. Garrett shook his head. "No," he replied. "It is just, at first when we met, I thought Ross and you to have been in love. I had questioned it before."

Georgia laughed. "How silly of you to think so!" she proclaimed teasingly.

"I believe I was actually envious of yours and his relationship."

"That is a new experience," she pointed out.

"What is?"

"A man envious of another man's attentions for me." She smirked.

"How do you think I felt when I heard you were engaged to Mr. Janes?"

"Oh, do not mention that again," she begged. "It is over and done with. There is nothing to fear from him!"

He chuckled.

"Might I ask you a question?"

He creased his brow in slight confusion. "Of course. You can always ask me anything."

She laughed through her nose. "I shall remember that when we are married for a certain number of years, and you start to become cross with me at all of my silly inquiries."

He laughed too.

"But, in all seriousness, what made you fall in love me?" she ventured a little tentatively.

Mr. Garrett took her hand and kissed it as he thought. "I feel as if I can be vulnerable around you," he told her almost without pausing to think. "My want or need to impress seems unnecessary when I am with you."

"Why should you ever feel the need to impress anyone?" Georgia asked, frowning slightly. "That is what is wrong with people. We have this need and desire to prove to others that we are better than them, and when we fall short of whom we try to portray ourselves to be, we are devastated, angry even."

Mr. Garrett smiled and laughed through his nose.

"Why do we torture ourselves for the sake of others who are just as likely to be leading a glamorous façade as we are?" she continued. "It is, and should be, perfectly fine to be ourselves."

"There it is," he said softly.

Georgia gave him a confused look. "There is what?"

"That confidence I often see in you. It is what I first found so intriguing about you. It led the foundation to what later became love."

She blushed and looked away for a moment. "I suppose, in a way, you inspire confidence in me."

"Perhaps, I am the only one who sees it," he surmised. "When I first came to visit my aunt and uncle, you were the only young woman who was not thrown at me, or throwing herself at me. You always appeared calm where they giggled behind their fans."

"Oh, simpering girls are horrid creatures, are they not?" she jested.

He laughed. "You joke, but they are. I much prefer them confident."

She grinned at him. "Then how lucky you are to have found me."

He gently took her by the hand, stopping her. "Yes," he agreed, placing his other hand on her cheek. "I do believe I am lucky."

Mr. Garrett gazed into her eyes, brightened by the flushing of her cheeks. He stroked her cheek with his thumb as he leaned in and pressed his lips against hers.

Epilogue

Georgia stared at the simple band on her ring finger and smiled, unable to believe how she could ever be so happy. Thinking back the past year or so and all of its failures and triumphs, she smiled warmly as she rubbed her swelling belly.

She took a deep breath and reached for her journal, her first gift from her husband. She opened it gently, staring at its blank pages for a few moments before dipping her peacock-feathered quill into the ink and bringing it down onto the paper, the tip scratching against its pages.

The young woman sighed, a shrill exhaling of air, as she looked out the window. "Is there not something romantic about the rain?" she asked to no one in particular.

Her elder sister glanced up at her over the brim of her book. "What are you talking about, Evangelina? How is the rain romantic?" she asked skeptically in return.

The young woman turned her head to look at her sister, her light brown curls bouncing about her head and still seeming to glow despite the lack of light in the room. "Oh, Georgia, you are too practical to understand," she teased.